LICENSED TO 1

Clandestine Affairs 3

Zara Chase

MENAGE EVERLASTING

Siren Publishing, Inc.
www.SirenPublishing.com

A SIREN PUBLISHING BOOK
IMPRINT: Ménage Everlasting

LICENSED TO THRILL
Copyright © 2014 by Zara Chase

ISBN: 978-1-62741-126-4

First Printing: April 2014

Cover design by Les Byerley
All art and logo copyright © 2014 by Siren Publishing, Inc.

Printed in the U.S.A.

PUBLISHER
Siren Publishing, Inc.
www.SirenPublishing.com

LICENSED TO THRILL

Clandestine Affairs 3

ZARA CHASE
Copyright © 2014

Chapter One

"What *is* your problem?"

Raoul shrugged. "Depends who you ask."

"Come on, man, keep up." Zeke shot Raoul a pissed look. "They're real babes, the pair of them."

Raoul gave the women in question a lazy once over. "I've seen worse."

"Earth to Raoul. Now is no time to get picky." Zeke rolled his eyes. "In case you missed the signals, they're hot for us, but they're also getting a lot of attention from other guys. We'll miss out if we don't make our move now."

Raoul took a long pull from his open bottle of beer, still watching the two women in question as they stood right in front of Raoul and Zeke, swaying their hips in time to the music being cranked out at an earsplitting level. He tried real hard to summon up some enthusiasm, but it just wasn't there.

"The brunette has possibilities." He shot Zeke a look. "Think she might be up for sharing us?"

"Doubt it. They look like they come as a package deal."

Raoul's halfhearted interest withered. "I'm gonna split, but you stay. Don't let me cramp your style."

"Nah, I ain't packing enough to keep 'em both happy."

Raoul hoisted a brow, amused. "At last the man admits to his shortcomings."

"Fuck off. There's nothing short about my God-given gifts." Zeke had to shout to make himself heard over the trio on stage in the packed bar. They were singing something about a long good-bye. It would be just fine by Raoul if they cut to the abbreviated version. "At least I'm still interested in getting laid, whereas your dick's in danger of dropping off from lack of use."

Raoul smirked. "And yours ain't?"

"What can I say?" Zeke shrugged. "One of us has to maintain the reputation we worked so hard to earn."

Raoul blinked at his buddy. "Why?"

"Why?" Zeke's eyes bugged. "Are you shitting me? These things matter, my friend. They matter a lot."

Raoul flapped a hand. "Yeah, if you say so."

"What is it, Raoul? What's eating you? I practically had to hogtie you just to get you to come into town. Now you're turning down fresh pussy when it's served up to you on a bone-china plate." Zeke tugged the end of his ponytail. "I just don't get it, man."

Raoul stood with his back to the bar, leaned both elbows on it, and watched the action going down, totally unimpressed by all the hustling, ducking, and diving. "What's the point of it all, Zeke? Have you ever stopped to ask yourself that?"

"Shit, now he's going all philosophical on me." Zeke shook his head. "This is worse than I thought. You really do need to get laid, buddy. You sure that sweet little brunette wouldn't take your mind off the greater meaning of life?"

"Doubt it." Raoul sighed. "When did women get to be so predatory? Call me old-fashioned, but I liked it in the days when the man made the running."

"You've been out of the game for too long, old man. Take my advice, and get back up on the horse before you forget how to ride."

Raoul gave the brunette another speculative glance, and chuckled. "Bareback?"

Zeke wagged a finger at him. "Safe sex, Mr. Washington. Safe sex."

"In which case, I'll pass."

A guy pushed past Raoul to get to the bar, spilling the dregs from his almost-empty glass over Raoul's boots without bothering to apologize.

"That's it." Raoul levered himself away from the bar. "I'm out of here. You coming?"

"Yeah, I guess." Zeke expelled a heavy sigh. "Shit, that blonde was hot."

"Hey, like I said, don't let me stop you."

"No, you're right, it ain't worth the effort. But I hear there's a new BDSM club opening up in town. We need to check that out sometime soon."

"Okay, that might work."

"That's what I like about you, bud. Your enthusiasm is infectious."

Raoul laughed and slapped Zeke's shoulder. As soon as they stepped outside into the almost-full parking lot Raoul gratefully swallowed down several mouthfuls of sweet Wyoming night air. That was more like it. A bar packed full of sweaty bodies, bad music played too loud, people pushing and shoving, predatory women eyeing him up—none of that shit did it for Raoul anymore. Zeke was probably right. He must be getting old.

Before they reached their truck, Raoul's cell rang. The caller's name was withheld, but few people had his private number so he took the call.

"Washington," he said abruptly.

"Raoul, this is Paul Bisset."

"Hey, Paul, how's it going?"

"Not so bad. Listen, I'm stuck at the Pentagon, but I have a problem. The sort of problem that made me immediately think of you."

Raoul frowned. He and Zeke had served with Paul in a previous life when they were all Green Berets—the elite of the elite. Raoul and Zeke left the service, but Paul had signed on for the long haul. A career soldier and natural diplomat, Paul was now a colonel, one of the youngest men to achieve that rank. For once the powers that be had promoted a man on merit, and now Paul was taking on the old school within the higher echelons of the Pentagon, playing military politics with the hand of a master. Raoul was glad there was someone in there fighting for his old comrades—someone who had been at the sharp end, put the serving men first, and didn't talk out of his ass. Raoul had a great deal of respect for Paul. He was tough, intelligent, and didn't take shit from anyone.

So why was Mr. Fixit calling Raoul out of the blue with unsolvable problems?

"Okay, what can I do for you?"

"It's my little sister, Jodie. You remember her?"

Raoul shook his head, even though Paul couldn't see the gesture. "Sorry, can't say that I do."

"Well, it was ten years ago when you met her. She was only twelve at the time, so I don't suppose she made much of an impression."

Raoul vaguely recalled a leggy colt with pigtails, a freckled nose, and endless questions following Paul and Raoul everywhere they went. "She the one who fell out of a tree, almost landed on my head, and then blamed me when she sprained her wrist?"

Paul chuckled. "That would be Jodie. But she ain't twelve anymore, and she's in way more trouble than getting stuck up a tree."

"Tell me."

"She's in London, England, and has gotten herself arrested."

"Oh." Raoul wondered what he was supposed to do about that. "Sounds like she needs a lawyer."

"Yeah, but it's delicate. I haven't told the old man yet, but he'll go ballistic when he hears."

"Ah, I see." Raoul immediately joined the dots. Paul's father was a hardliner—tough on crime, tough on immigration, tough on just about every damned thing, including his kids. He was now running for the senate, and if word of his only daughter's arrest got out it would probably kill his campaign stone dead. "What did Jodie do this time?"

"She's a real crusader. Always fighting for the underdog."

"Yes, and..." Raoul had a nasty feeling. "What precisely was she arrested for, Paul?"

"Er, it's bad, buddy." Raoul heard him swallow. "She's been arrested under the Terrorism Act."

A chill ran down Raoul's spine. "The British Terrorism Act?"

"Yeah, which amounts to terrorism against America, too, because the two countries are joined at the hip politically when it comes to that sort of stuff."

"What the fuck has she been up to?"

Paul's sigh echoed down the line. "She isn't too sure herself. I gotta tell you, Raoul, she might be a bit wild, but she's no terrorist. It has to be a setup. Someone getting to the old man through her."

Raoul took a moment to process what Paul had told him. It had to be more than that, and whatever it was, it wasn't just Paul's father who would suffer from the consequences. It wouldn't reflect well on Paul either, what with his sensitive position within the Pentagon. If his enemies found out, it would give them the perfect opportunity to oust him.

"I don't know any more than that," Paul said into the silence. "Jodie called me, sounding scared, but said she had no idea what it was all about. There were a bunch of them in a house somewhere. It was raided, and they were all arrested."

"So it might not be her they're after?"

"No, but if someone else in that house was into something anti-establishment she'll be implicated, too, especially given her background. Anyway, I told her to sit tight and say nothing until I got her a lawyer."

"Has the American embassy gotten involved?"

"She was allowed only one call, which she made to me. I haven't told the embassy, but they'll get to hear of it sooner or later, you can bet your life on that. I wanted to try and get her out, and fix it all, before the old man hears about it."

"When the embassy finds out she's in custody, surely they'll be obliged to step in to see if they can help?"

"They would if Jodie asked for them to, I guess, but in cases as sensitive as this, particularly with the old man being in the position he's in, they'll probably bury their heads and see how it plays out."

I'll just bet they will. "Spoken like a true cynic."

"Just telling you what I know they'll be thinking."

"Okay, I see, but I still don't—"

"I have to try and save Jodie from her own stupidity. She's no fucking terrorist, Raoul, just a woman with an overdeveloped conscience who thinks she can right all the world's wrongs single-handed."

Raoul rolled his eyes. "Of course she is."

"I'd go to London myself, but I simply can't leave right now. We've got some high-powered discussions going on about…well, I can't tell you what about, but I need to be there. Trust me, if I didn't then I would—"

"Okay," Raoul said. "I might know someone who can help."

"That would be awesome." Raoul could hear the relief in Paul's voice. "I owe you big time, buddy. It's only a matter of time before someone tells the old man. I'd like to know what's going on and be able to break the news to him myself."

"Where's Jodie being held?"

"Paddington Green, central London."

"That figures." Raoul thought fast. That was where they took all British terror suspects. "Okay, hang in there. I'll get back to you, soon as I know anything."

Raoul cut the connection. Zeke already had the truck fired up. He backed it out of the lot, heading in the direction of their ranch, all thoughts of getting laid put aside. Raoul brought him up to speed while he drove.

"Don't like the sound of it," Zeke said. "The Brits don't arrest Americans for no reason."

"She's obviously gotten herself into something that could come back and bite Paul's dad on the ass." Raoul curled his upper lip. "Paul's real worried about his baby sister, but it sounded like their old man's only concern, once he finds out about it, will be for his career."

"He's a politician. What else would you expect?"

"Yeah, right." Raoul kicked moodily at the mat in the footwell of their truck.

"Who we got over there?"

Raoul and Zeke ran a clandestine agency, manned by tough ex-forces guys, that couldn't be found in any phone directory. A lot of their assignments came from the military hierarchy, who couldn't be seen to get involved in sorting out their own screw-ups. Others came from contacts like Paul. Raoul's operatives worked under the radar, obeying no one's dictates other than those of their own consciences. They had all experienced the horrors and injustices of war firsthand, and were now ready to redress the balance, one case at a time.

"Milo and Hal," Raoul said. "Milo has a law degree, as well as being hard-ass ex-SAS—"

Zeke smirked. "What, those SAS wimps who think they measure up to us Green Berets?"

"They do, and you well know it. I seem to recall that time when one of those SAS wimps kicked your ass on the assault course."

"Just one time," Zeke protested. "And I had the hangover from hell that day."

Raoul laughed. "Anyway, this ought to suit Milo and Hal down to the ground."

"I don't like the sound of it, Raoul. Terrorism?" Zeke shook his head. "The Brits don't usually get that stuff wrong."

"Yeah, I hear you."

As soon as Raoul got into his state-of-the-art office, he picked up his secure phone and called his buddies in London. It would be four in the morning there, but Milo wouldn't mind about that.

Chapter Two

A jackhammer pounded away at the inside of Milo's skull like it bore him a personal grudge. A jackhammer with a ring tone—that was a new one. What the fuck had they put in those damned shots? He groaned, pulling the covers over his head, trying to block out the pain and the noise. This was it. He'd played his luck once too often, had died, and gone straight to hell.

The pounding and ringing endured. Yep, definitely hell. He reluctantly forced his eyes open, and returned to a semiconscious state. Shit, his phone was ringing. He sat up and scrubbed a hand down his face, so wasted he now seriously wished he *was* dead. Hell hadn't seemed all that bad. He peered bleary-eyed at the clock. Four thirty in the morning. What the fuck! He'd only got to bed—well, to his own bed—a couple of hours ago. Who would be calling him so early?

He reached for his phone and took the call without checking to see who it was. Anything to shut off the persistent noise.

"This had fucking better be good."

"Evening, Milo."

"It might be evening in fucking Wyoming, but it's the middle of the night here. What's so fucking urgent, Raoul?"

"Glad to hear your sense of humor's alive and kicking."

"About the only fucking part of me that is. What do you want that can't wait until a more civilized hour?"

"Sister of a friend has gone and gotten herself arrested—"

"And that would interest me because…"

"They've taken her to Paddington Green."

The fog inside Milo's brain began to clear. "Ah, terrorist charges, I take it."

"That's what I need you to find out."

Milo sighed, grabbed a pen, and prayed for his gut to stop churning. How much booze exactly had he and Hal put away earlier? No, better not to think about it, or the two chicks they'd hooked up with afterward. Big mistake, that. He'd only just escaped with his manhood intact when he'd insisted on returning home after they'd had their fun. Milo didn't do all-nighters, and women universally appeared to have a problem with that.

"Okay, bud, hit me with the details."

"The lady in question is known to you."

"Uh-huh. I didn't do it."

Raoul laughed. "She's Paul Bisset's little sister."

Milo's sluggish brain clicked into a higher gear. "Not the kid we met a decade or so ago? The one who fell out of a tree, and nearly flattened the lot of us?" Milo managed a humorless laugh as he recalled the scene. Four hard-as-nails special services guys almost wiped out by a gangly kid. "Paul never stopped ribbing us about it."

"That would be the one. Except she's no longer a kid."

Milo grunted. "If she got herself arrested on terrorist charges then she's still thinking like one."

Five minutes later Milo cut the connection, reckoned he could be excused for indulging in another aggrieved sigh, and then hit the shower. He was more than happy to help people in distress, when that distress was genuine. That's why half the legal work he did was pro bono. But a poor little rich girl, playing with fire because she actually *wanted* to get burned, didn't float Milo's boat. He shook his head, resisting the urge to snarl. He owed Paul a favor, and could never say *no* to Raoul, otherwise…

In a foul state of mind, Milo knew he would be no good to anyone until he sobered up completely. He stood under the steaming hot jets, and closed his eyes as the water bounced off the top of his aching head and cascaded over the rest of him. He applied a liberal amount of bodywash to his hands and scrubbed his torso with considerable vigor, imagining the booze seeping out of his pores as he watched the grime accumulated during another pointless night flow down the drain.

It was a bit like the direction his life had taken, in some respects. He'd been restless since getting out of the SAS, and practicing law just wasn't cutting it for him. Way too many rules and regulations in this fine country, all tilted in favor of the criminal. That's why he'd been happy to sign on as one of Raoul's merry band of vigilantes, but when doing so he hadn't reckoned on being asked to babysit a poor little rich kid with more time on her hands than she knew what to do with.

"Whoa there, you're jumping to conclusions," he said aloud, but his instincts seldom let him down and he was pretty sure his assessment of Ms. Bisset was right on the money.

Feeling only fractionally better after several minutes of near sauna-like temperatures, he turned the tap to cold and endured the freezing spray for a full sixty seconds. Stepping out of the stall, shivering and swearing, Milo toweled himself dry and cleaned a patch of steam from the mirror with his hand. His expression reflected his annoyance, his eyes looked bloodshot, and he needed a shave. There was nothing he could do about his eyes, and he couldn't be arsed to attend to his stubbly chin, or his attitude, either. He'd just have to do.

Milo pulled on a pair of worn jeans, padded barefoot and bare-chested into the main part of the loft he shared with Hal, and fired up his laptop. Then he typed in the name of his soon-to-be-client to see what edifying information St. Google could provide him with. While he waited, he thumped on Hal's door. Hard. No response.

"Come on, mate." He walked into Hal's room, and was almost asphyxiated by the smell of stale booze. He waved a hand beneath his nose and moved across to the window, throwing it wide open. "Rise and shine. Sleep's overrated."

The mound beneath the covers groaned. "Fuck off!"

"We got a shout from across the pond."

"Give Uncle Sam my best."

Milo shook Hal's shoulder. "We need to move on this, pal."

Hal rolled over, and opened one eye that resembled the map of a small banana republic. He sent Milo a look that would have shrunk a lesser man's balls. "You have got to be shitting me."

"The client's young, female, and hot."

Milo was unsure if the hot bit was actually true, but it had the desired effect. Hal blinked, processed what Milo had told him, then pushed back the covers and made a manly effort to stand up. He managed it on the third attempt, his colorful language turning the stale air in his bedroom blue.

"Hit the shower, my friend. Your personal hygiene could use some work."

Hal shot him the finger. "Give me five." His blond hair stuck up from his head at unnatural angles. He ran a hand through it as he shuffled toward his bathroom, still mumbling and complaining. "And you'd better not be putting me on."

"As if."

Milo went back to his computer, but found precious little of interest about Jodie Bisset. He found a whole load of stuff about her father and brother, though, which got him wondering. Anyone with terrorist tendencies, living in England and known to the authorities, would be flagged, just like they were in the States. Raoul hadn't been able to find anything on Jodie his end. Milo ran a program he wasn't supposed to even know existed, much less have access to, and discovered that England's security services didn't have anything on her, either.

"Something ain't right," he said aloud.

"Yeah, like dragging me out of bed at five in the morning." Hal wandered into the room, towel-drying his hair. "What's happening?"

Milo filled him in.

"Sounds like a setup to me." Hal helped himself to a mug of the fresh coffee Milo had just brewed. "Someone wants to discredit daddy dearest. English politics are a cake walk compared to the dirty tricks they get up to over *there.*"

"This chick, Jodie, is out to right all the world's wrongs, apparently," Milo replied, stifling a yawn.

"That young, eh?"

"Twenty-two."

"Well, we'd best get over there and see what we can do for the idealistic little love," Hal grumbled.

"I called the nick and told them I was her legal representative. They didn't like it. Said she hadn't asked for anyone, but now they can't use the thumbscrews on her without us being there."

"Why do I have to hold your hand? You're the hot-shot lawyer. You could have left me in bed."

"Because, if this is a setup, we're gonna have to find out why, and who's behind it. And you, Mr. Lewis, much as it pains me to admit it, are a kick-arse investigator."

"Yeah, yeah, whatever."

"No point in getting to the nick before seven. The people that matter won't be there before then, so they'll only leave us to kick our heels."

"So why the fuck did you get me out of bed?"

"Need to use those contacts of yours, mate. See if you can find out what the charge is, and why Jodie was pulled in, who else was arrested with her, who gave the tip-off. She ain't on the security services' radar, so someone somewhere pulled a number."

"How did I know that was what you were going to say?"

Milo sent his buddy a droll glance. "Lucky guess."

An hour later, the two guys set off from their Battersea apartment, headed for Paddington Green, looking as though they'd just slept eight hours straight. That was what the tough training it took to be accepted into the SAS did for a guy. They had learned to eat and sleep whenever the opportunity arose, and knew how to be awake and alert—more or less—within seconds of that necessity arising. The only sign that Milo wasn't at his most alert was a slight limp, which annoyed the fuck out of him. He had spent more hours than he cared to think about getting past a disability he refused to acknowledge, but sometimes it defied his best efforts to remain hidden.

They were now in possession of a lot more information regarding Jodie Bisset's arrest, and Milo wasn't happy about what he'd learned. It smelt like a clumsy setup, but just by getting herself arrested, the damage was already done for the Bisset family. Even if Jodie was subsequently acquitted, a question mark would always hang over her activities.

"Don't forget," Milo said as they stepped through the doors to the station. "You're my assistant."

Hal shot him a disgruntled look. "Assistant?"

Mil managed a brief grin. "Don't get your panties in a wad. They won't let you see our client unless you're part of her legal team."

* * * *

Jodie sat on the edge of the rock-hard bunk, cuddling her arms around her torso in a vain attempt to ward off the pre-dawn chill. Not that she was cold, but she couldn't seem to stop trembling. The tiny cell assigned to her smelt of urine, fear, and desperation—and she could definitely relate to the fear part. How had this happened to her? What was she doing here in this crappy cell, accused of being behind all sorts of scary, subversive activities? She was shit scared, and knew her bluster hadn't fooled anyone into thinking otherwise. She had no idea how long she had been here. It was early afternoon, she thought, when armed police—armed police in England!—crashed through the door of the Camden Town house where she'd been plotting the following day's activities with the rest of the group. They had all been handcuffed, and frog-marched out of there, no explanation given, and bundled into the back of a police van.

When she was told they were being taken to Paddington Green police station, she almost peed her pants. This was serious. It was where they brought all the hard cases—the terrorists. She had gone through the humiliation of being fingerprinted, photographed, and strip-searched by an overenthusiastic butch female cop. Mercifully, she'd been allowed to keep her own clothes once they'd finished with her. She'd been asked lots of questions, but wouldn't answer any of them, mainly because she couldn't. The cops tried the old trick of saying her friends were talking up a storm, blaming everything on her. Jodie didn't buy it because she hadn't done anything for them to blame her for.

She insisted upon making a phone call, and rang Paul collect back in the States. He would know what to do. She blocked her father from her mind completely, caring as much about him as he ever had about her—as he had about anything except his precious career. Paul had said he'd get help for her, and she knew he'd come through. It was just a case of when. In the meantime, she continued to sit tight and remained tight-lipped. The cops eventually got tired of goading her, and sent her back to this cell.

They'd given her something unrecognizable to eat, but her stomach rebelled at the very thought of ingesting food. They gave her a weak liquid as gray as the walls of her cell, masquerading as tea. She hadn't touched that, either. She was empty inside, frightened, alone, and a little bit angry—at herself for being so gullible—but she saved most of her anger for whoever had landed her in this mess. She didn't believe any of her buddies were terrorists. They were just young people with strong views and consciences who wanted to make a difference in this world. What was so bad about that? Wasn't it what young people were supposed to do, before they settled down, accepted the system, and became model citizens who criticized young people?

Okay, so one or two of her lot *were* very opinionated, but she would know if they had extreme tendencies, wouldn't she? Still, how well did one person really know another? Wasn't that how terrorist cells integrated themselves into the fabric of society?

Oh hell, was that what had happened to her?

Jodie told herself repeatedly that *she* was guilty of nothing more sinister than wanting to make the world a better place. The problem was, if someone had set her up to get to her dad, they would have had the clout to do a decent job of it. They would have planted a shedload of evidence against her, and no one would believe she was innocent. At least not until her dad's chances of being elected to the senate were well and truly blown by his only daughter's illegal activities. Mud sticks.

Jodie disciplined herself to stop panicking. Sleeping in this horrible place was out of the question, so she might as well apply her mind to the problem and try to figure out what was going on. She ran through her friends in her head, one by one, thinking hard about their backgrounds, and what she knew about them as individuals.

Not that much, when it came down to it. They all had the same ideals, were prepared to do what it took to get their campaigns noticed, even if that required them to flirt with the shady side of the law. They were committed, and that was all she'd ever needed to know. She didn't particularly like some of them, and couldn't imagine being friends with them, but that wasn't what this was about. A couple of the guys had come on to her. She'd turned them down, and they didn't seem to bear a grudge. Anyway, they'd been arrested along with everyone else. No, there had to be something else. Something she was missing.

She hadn't gotten anywhere trying to figure out what it might be, when she heard the jangling sound of a bunch of keys. Obviously not more food then. That was delivered through a shoot, in the same way caged animals in zoos were sometimes fed. For some reason, that thought angered her more than her current dilemma. To be treated as though she was a dangerous animal whom no human could risk direct contact with was the ultimate humiliation.

An officer stepped into her humble abode, and looked her over with an expression of scathing contempt.

"Your brief's here," he said blandly.

"My what?"

"Oh yeah, you're a Yank. Excuse me, your lawyer's here."

At last! Paul had obviously come through for her, but the damned lawyer had taken his time getting here.

"What time is it?" she asked.

"Seven in the morning." The officer leered at her. "Why are you so interested? Got somewhere you need to be?"

"What, and deprive myself of these salubrious accommodations?" Jodie resisted the urge to flip him the bird. "How could I possibly walk away?"

His leer turned into a smug grin. "I very much doubt if you'll get the chance anytime soon."

That's what Jodie was so worried about. She stood up, trying to look unconcerned as she followed the officer from the room, along a dingy corridor, and up a flight of steps, pausing for him to unlock another door when they reached the top. They didn't handcuff her, which was something, she supposed.

The officer opened the door to a small, windowless room and stood back to let Jodie walk through it ahead of him. He then closed the door, and Jodie found herself alone with two men. She glanced up and gasped. The taller of the two had a shock of thick black hair that fell across his brow. He wore a well-tailored suit over a black mesh T-shirt, and intelligent gray eyes assessed her, appearing to miss little. He was a very good-looking man, with a strong, square jaw sporting a day's worth of stubble. His face hinted at tough resourcefulness, his hard body radiated animal vitality. He was the type of guy who would instantly make anyone feel less anxious. He was ex-military.

Of course he was.

Jodie knew it for a fact, and would have recognized him anywhere. It was twelve years since she had last seen him, but images of his handsome face had haunted her dreams ever since. She knew his name before he even introduced himself. Milo Hanson had ridden to her rescue, just as he had done so often in her aforementioned dreams. She hadn't known he was a lawyer, but should have guessed it. She immediately felt a whole lot better. If anyone could help her, it was Milo.

Jodie felt grubby, and uncharacteristically unsure of herself, as gray eyes continued to assess her. And those eyes didn't look particularly impressed by what they saw. She could hardly blame him for that, and was grateful he didn't seem to recognize her. She was wearing comfortable old jeans, a tatty university sweatshirt, and hadn't washed her hair in two days. Prison grime clung to her like a second skin, the difference between their respective appearances emphasized by his pristine clothing, and the firm set to his gorgeous lips. He clearly wasn't happy to be here, and Jodie couldn't entirely blame him for that.

She glanced at his companion, glad for a reason to avoid Milo's hostile gaze. The second guy was a little shorter than his buddy— perhaps an even six feet—with fabulous dirty-blond hair, piercing blue eyes, and, unlike Milo, a wayward smile that implied approval, imbuing her with a shot of much-needed confidence. He was dressed in jeans and a T-shirt, and looked like he'd just gotten out of bed. Given the hour, he most likely had.

"Jodie Bisset?"

She nodded. "Last time I checked."

"I'm Milo Hanson." He threw a business card at her. She picked it up and saw that nowadays he made his living as a partner in what they called a solicitors' office on this side of the pond. Unlike Paul, he'd obviously gotten out of the military. "Your brother asked me to come get you out of here."

"Can you do that?" she asked a little too anxiously.

"Not sure yet." He waved toward the other guy. "This is my investigator, Hal Lewis."

Hal offered her his hand, which was more than Milo had done. His grasp was firm, and as his long fingers engulfed her palm the contact sent an unexpected spiral of lust straight to her pussy. Hell, now wasn't the time!

"Nice meeting you," Hal said, giving her an up-close view of sparkling white, very even teeth. "Wish it could have been under different circumstances."

She rolled her eyes. "You and me both."

"Let's get started." Milo pointed to a chair, which Jodie took, and he then sat across from her. Hal sat to his right with a pad open in front of him. "Do you know what they've charged you with?"

"Something to do with terrorism?" She shook her head. "They weren't too specific, and I was too shocked to push them. But you need to know, Mr. Hanson—"

"Call me Milo."

"Okay, Milo, you need to know I'm about as likely to commit acts of terrorism as your queen is to go limbo dancing."

Hal's lips twitched, but Milo didn't crack a smile. "Then why are you here?"

"Wish I knew." Jodie shrugged. "Can't help thinking it might be something to do with my dad. You know about him?"

"We've met."

Of course they had. Jodie wanted to remind Milo that they'd met before as well, but refrained. He was all business, and so ought she to be. This was her freedom at stake here, but she still couldn't help thinking that Milo was even more devastatingly handsome than she recalled. Hal was, too. Milo was dressed like a businessman, while Hal, in worn jeans and T-shirt, looked like he was heading for the beach. The contrast was mind-blowing. If the two of them went out, hunting as a pack, the girls would flock them like hounds following a scent.

Remember that, and stop acting like a lovesick kid.

"Someone, somewhere, doesn't want Dad and his radical views elected to the senate," she said quickly, flushing when she realized she'd been gawping at them. "Can't say as I blame them for that, but I take exception to them using me as their conduit."

"Seems a bit extreme." Milo hoisted one brow in an adorable gesture that only served to heighten his good looks. It also made it clear that he didn't believe her, which infuriated Jodie.

"Not really," she replied acerbically. "The entire western world is paranoid about acts of terrorism, given our recent history, so they tend to overreact if they get a tip-off. And a tip is all they would need, isn't it?"

"Very likely." Hal leaned back in his chair, legs splayed, like they were chatting about nothing more important than the weather. "Might be tough finding out whom, though."

Whom? Aw, gotta love the English! "Do we need to do that? Isn't it enough just to prove I'm innocent?"

"Ordinarily, yes," Milo replied. "But the powers that be tend to get a bit twitchy if the word *terrorism* is used. With good reason, as it happens."

"Do I look like a terrorist?" she demanded.

"Describe a terrorist's look," Milo shot back.

"Calm down, children," Hal said, waving a placating hand. "We're on your side, honey, but we won't be much use to you if we don't get the whole picture."

"Right, so let's start at the beginning." Milo leaned slightly toward her. She caught a whiff of his bodywash, fresh spicy cologne, and hot, sexy male. The aroma was as out of place in this dreary dump as the man himself was. "Tell me everything. If I'm to help you, then I need to know it all."

"In what respect?"

"What group were you mixed up with when they came for you? What were you planning? The whole works."

Chapter Three

"Where to start?"

Milo looked up from the papers he had in front of him and sent her a wry glance that said, *don't waste my time.* "The beginning's usually a pretty good place," he said curtly.

He examined their client closely while she assembled her thoughts. The freckles he remembered still decorated the bridge of her nose, standing out in stark contrast to the pallor of her skin. She obviously didn't remember him, which was probably for the best. He wondered if she was actually guilty, figuring she was involved to some degree, even if she wasn't aware of it. Someone like her, young, American, idealistic, and full of naïve fervor to make a difference, would be a prime target for ambitious terrorist groups.

He refused to be impressed by her physical attributes, evident even through her rumpled clothing, and after a night in the cells. Typically, Hal showed no such restraint, and smiled at her with unreserved approval. Under different circumstances Milo might have done the same thing. He and Hal were typically drawn to the same type of woman, and Jodie was definitely their type—physically at least. But as far as Milo was concerned, her philosophy sucked.

He and Hal had seen more than their fair share of war zones, and the brutality that went with those conflicts. He didn't need crusading types who knew little or nothing about the realities of those war-torn, far-flung countries sticking their oar in, muddying the waters, pretending they knew what was best. Still, she was young, so he tried to remain professional, and cut her some slack. Presumably she was rebelling against her old man, or whatever the hell it was that kids did for kicks nowadays.

And from Milo's perspective, she *was* a kid. At twenty-two, she was ten years, and way too many unpleasant experiences, younger than he was. She had to be five seven, and had long, thick, brunette hair, in need of a wash, held back with a colored band. Her face was dominated by a pair of huge brown eyes—eyes that defied her tough attitude and gave away just how scared she was to find herself in this place. Scared was good. It tended to concentrate the mind. Milo ought to know. She had high cheekbones, delicate brows, and a pouty mouth that cried out to be kissed. *Don't go there, Hanson!*

"We were planning to stage a demonstration outside the Syrian embassy tomorrow," she said, pulling Milo out of his erotic reverie.

"Just a minute. Who's we?"

"A group of us who care about all those displaced people," she replied passionately. "Someone has to do something."

Perhaps, but Milo knew a demonstration would make the sum difference of none whatsoever. "How many of you were involved in organizing this protest?" he asked.

"Six."

"Can you give me their names, and as much information about them as you know?"

"Why?" She shook her head. "None of them are terrorists."

Give me strength! "Look," Milo said, leaning in close, invading her personal space. "I've had two hours' sleep, and am not in the mood to be pissed about. If you want my help, then you need to answer my questions. British police get it wrong, just like they do on your side of the pond, but they still wouldn't have raided that house in Camden Town without good reason."

"Now just a goddamned minute. Are you saying—"

Milo held up a hand, cutting her off mid-flow. "You really figure someone did this to get back at your old man?"

Her eyes widened. "I already told you that."

"It's a possibility," Hal said. "But this Syrian thing isn't your only cause, is it?"

"Well no, now you mention it, it was a spur-of-the-moment thing to get involved."

Milo sent her a probing look. "Yeah, and who spurred your moment?"

"One of the organizers. I know him from other causes."

"I need their names," Hal said, pen poised. "That would be a good place to start."

"They wouldn't!"

"If you're right about your old man's enemies, then someone sure as hell would," Milo replied. "Either someone inside your group is working against you—"

"Never!"

"Then let's have their names, and nationalities."

"Now you're just being racist."

Milo smothered a sigh. *God save me from politically correct activists.* "Do you want my help or not?"

She laced the fingers of one hand through those of the other, folded them neatly in her lap, and expelled a deep sigh. "I'm sorry," she said, avoiding eye contact. "I didn't sleep much either, surprising as it might seem, but I am very grateful you're here."

"Okay then, let's hear it all."

Milo studied her body language as intently as he listened to the words that spilled from her lips. It quickly became evident that she didn't know a whole lot about her fellow activists. In some cases she didn't even know their surnames. That didn't matter. Milo would be able to extract all that information from the arrest record. He was just curious to discover how deeply Ms. Bisset was committed to her cause.

Very deeply, it would appear. She launched into a lecture about the evils of Sadat's regime, the dangers of egomaniacs having too much control over the countries they ruled, the plight of displaced refugees…

"Who owns the house in Camden Town?" Milo asked, cutting across her diatribe.

"Oh, Phil and Betty rent it. It's the hub of a whole lot of activities. People come and go all the time." She shrugged. "It's kinda open house, I guess."

"They are the two who came up with the idea for the protest outside the embassy, and recruited you?"

"No, that was Jeff."

"Who's Jeff?" Hal asked, scribbling away.

"We've been involved in other causes together, and keep each other informed about what's going on. There's a chat room as well, where notices are put up, so like-minded people know what's happening."

"Great," Milo muttered. "Rent-a-demo is all we need."

"I wouldn't expect an establishment man like you to understand."

"You and this Jeff are an item?" Milo ignored the stab of jealousy that pierced his gut. Geez, he really must be tired. Jodie was a babe, but even if she wasn't a client, he wouldn't…her ideals, her beliefs, just didn't jibe with his own thinking. *Yeah, just keep telling yourself that.*

"No, just fellow activists."

"Okay," Milo said, when it became apparent that Jodie had nothing further of interest to tell him. "What do you know about Spectrum?"

"What?"

She showed absolutely no signs of recognition, and Milo had been watching carefully for them. He'd shot the question at her out of the blue, hoping for a reaction. Either she really was in the dark, or she was the best actress this side of Hollywood.

"It's a terrorist cell operating in this country that the security services have had their eye on for some time."

Jodie shook her head. "Well, you know more than I do. Hand on heart, I've never heard of them, and if I had, I would have steered well clear. I'm into peaceful protest, not blowing up innocent people in pursuit of a misguided cause."

Milo believed her—at least about that. "Hal did a bit of research before we came over here," he said.

"I wondered what kept you."

Milo's anger won out over discretion. *Talk about gratitude!* "I'm sorry if we kept you waiting too long," he said, twisting his lips into a cynical knot.

"You're being paid to help me, aren't you?"

Milo merely shook his head, wondering if she could possibly imagine how close he was to walking out on her.

"I'm sorry," she said, flushing. "I guess I'm a bit on edge. I've never been arrested before. It's not an experience I would recommend."

It was Hal who broke the tension. "Chill, babe," he said in his usual laidback manner. "It's no wonder you're on edge, but try to keep the anger caged."

"Just so that you know," Milo said in an icy tone. "We came to try and help you because a friend, your brother, asked us to. Money doesn't come into it."

"Look, I've said I'm sorry. Can we keep my big mouth out of it, and talk about getting me out of this shithole."

"Okay, here's the deal." Milo drilled her with a look. "The police found literature in the house they reckon they can connect to Spectrum. Worse, they found details of a planned firebombing of a club in Mayfair. It's a club that has a lot of rich Syrian ex-pats as members. They support the Sadat regime with money, and other resources."

Once again Jodie shook her head. A long strand of hair had escaped from her ponytail, filling Milo with an irrational urge to release the rest, just so that he could see it tumble around her slim shoulders. What the fuck was wrong with him?

"There's nothing more I can add to what I've already said. I know nothing about Spectrum, and if anyone in that house does then they didn't share. What's more, like I already said, if I had known, I would have walked out. I don't do violence." She folded her arms defensively beneath her breasts, pushing them against the fabric of her sweatshirt, giving Milo a clear view of two ripe babies just begging to be sucked—or clamped, or bitten, or…fuck, he had to stay focused here. "I leave that kind of stuff to the men in my family."

Milo shared a glance with Hal, knowing their thoughts would be running along similar lines. Jodie obviously resented what her brother did for a living, and what her father stood for. Her pioneering causes were her way of fighting back.

"I'll swear on a stack of bibles, take a lie detector test, whatever it takes to get out of here," she said on a tone of faint injury.

"How come you're living in London?" Milo asked.

"I've lived all over the world, never in one place for more than five minutes." Jodie's expression was resentful. "No friends, no continuity, because we were never in one place for long enough to establish roots. Well, I guess you guys know where I'm coming from."

"What makes you say that?" Milo asked.

"Come on, you have military stamped all over you."

"Yeah, okay, I know it can be tough on families," Milo said, his stance momentarily softening. "Hell, it's tough on the soldiers, too, but someone has to keep the rest of the world safe."

"Dad was a diplomat." She shrugged. "Still is. He left the soldiering to Paul, who toed the family line and did as he was told."

"Unlike you?"

"Someone has to be the black sheep." She sent them a brief, wicked smile that did all sorts of strange things to Milo—mainly his cock, which stood up and took a keen interest in the proceedings.

"Dad was posted to embassies all over the world, and Mom and I tagged along. Paul's a lot older than me, and was already in the military by the time I reached the age to wonder about these things." She stretched and settled into a more comfortable position—if that was possible—on the hard plastic chairs provided. "Dad finished up in London when I was fifteen. I started making career choices so I could decide what subjects to specialize in at school, but suddenly it was time to go back to the States, permanently. I didn't want to, dug my toes in, and was allowed to stay and finish my education. I went on to university at Cambridge."

Milo was impressed. In spite of the university system having been dumbed down over the years, Cambridge still maintained high standards and took only the brightest and best.

"What did you read?" he asked.

"History and politics."

That figured. "And do you have a job here in England? Is that why you stayed?"

"I stayed because I like England. And yes, I do have a job. I'm a researcher for a historian in Cambridge. He never leaves the town, and hates doing his own research. So I find what he needs, either online or in the great libraries here in London, and send it on to him."

"And that pays enough for you to live on?" Milo asked skeptically.

"I work part time in a bookstore in Covent Garden, too, and have a tiny studio apartment in Stockwell."

"Your family has money," Hal remarked. "Don't they help you out?"

"Dad wants me to go back to the States." She shrugged. "I don't."

Milo quirked a brow. "So he withholds funding?"

"I don't need his charity." She tossed her head. "I can make my own way."

Milo allowed his glance to rest on the grimy walls of the interview room they occupied and said nothing.

"Yes, well, normally I can."

"Presumably your academic in Cambridge would vouch for your character," Milo said.

"I'm sure he would."

"Okay, that's something. Now, the police want to talk to you again, and I think you should tell them everything they want to know. I'll be there, and if I think a question is inappropriate I'll tell you not to answer it. But, the more open you are with them, the less likely they are to think you're involved."

"And if I do that, will they let me go?"

"They have forty-eight hours under the Prevention of Terrorism Act to hold you. After that, they must either charge you or let you go. But, they can also apply to a magistrate for a twenty-four-hour extension so they can question you further. If you don't cooperate, that's a good enough reason to apply for that extension, and they would probably get it."

"I see."

"Let's tell them you're ready to talk, then we'll see. I think there's a good chance of getting you out, provided you lose the attitude, and answer them candidly. They have a job to do, same as anyone else."

"Is he always this bossy?" she asked Hal.

Hal grinned. "Baby, you have no idea!"

And such a question would earn her a good spanking, under normal circumstances. Just as well these circumstances were far from normal. Milo *so* didn't want to make this thing personal, but was already fighting a rearguard action. He glanced up at Jodie and happened to catch her magnetic gaze head-on. Her eyes widened as she caught him looking, and he felt himself drowning in their worried brown depths. It was the concern—the fragility, vulnerability, or whatever the hell it was—he detected beneath her tough exterior that so got to him. The urge to reach out and touch her, to make her understand she was no longer alone, was tough to resist.

Damn it, there was just something about her that compelled him, even if she was hopelessly idealistic, rude, and opinionated. He and Hal never had problems attracting women, and certainly didn't need the hassle of all the emotional baggage this one carried with her. So what if she appeared to be able to heat his blood, flame his passions, and make him consider throwing the rule book out the window.

He'd get over his mild obsession, and life would get back to normal.

* * * *

Ten minutes later Jodie sat in the same interview room she had been taken to before, only this time she wasn't alone. Milo's reassuring presence made all the difference in the world, even if he didn't appear to like her, or believe in her innocence. She had been allowed to use the restroom before the interview started, begged a comb from a sympathetic female guard, and splashed water over her face. She still felt like shit, but at least there was room for a little optimism now. She glanced at Milo's handsome profile, taking comfort from his intelligence and no-nonsense attitude. His body language exuded confidence, causing her to feel a whole lot better about the world. If she had to be in this situation, there was no one she would prefer to have fighting in her corner.

It was obvious Milo didn't want to be here, that he didn't much approve of her, or what she stood for. She had wasted more hours than was healthy imagining accidently bumping into him on the street and having him fall headlong in love with her. She glanced down at her shabby clothes, and expelled a cynical little laugh. Things couldn't have turned out more differently.

Milo was no longer the same person she remembered. He was harder, less willing to trust, as though his experiences as a soldier had altered him. Those experiences had left lines on his rugged features that added to his allure. His voice hadn't changed at all, though. She'd been twelve when she first heard his clipped, upper-class British accent. It had captivated her then, and had lost none of its ability to enthrall during the ensuing decade.

If only he would lighten up a bit. She knew the situation was serious, but she was innocent, and refused to believe she wouldn't walk out of here shortly, a free woman. The only sign that Milo had seen her as a woman was when their gazes had briefly clashed earlier. She saw something in his eyes then—interest, recognition— something other than derision. A kernel of unfamiliar sensation curled through her when he was slow to avert his gaze. Jodie realized then that she didn't give a shit what the authorities thought about her activities. She wouldn't lose any sleep if she screwed up her father's political career, either. All that mattered was that she somehow convince Milo and his hunky buddy Hal that she was not a terrorist.

Suddenly, nothing in this world mattered more.

"Ready?" he asked when the door opened and the same two detectives who had tried to grill her earlier took seats opposite them.

"As I ever will be."

"Don't worry. Just remember what we agreed."

Like I'd ever forget anything you said to me.

The detectives asked if Jodie minded the interview being recorded. Milo answered for her, saying they had no objections. Names, dates, and times were stated for the record. Then it began. She followed Milo's advice, keeping her responses short and to the point. She was acutely conscious of his muscled thigh, encased in exquisitely tailored pants, mere inches from her grubby jeans. She was sure she could feel the heat emanating from those thighs, seeping into her bones, and curling around her damaged heart. The strong, magnetic pull she felt toward a man who didn't like her very much— make that not at all—intensified. Heat invaded her gut whenever he glanced at her, and she was filled with renewed determination to say and do whatever he asked her to—even if it went against her beliefs— just to have him smile at her.

Milo let her speak for herself, only interrupting very occasionally if the detectives went too far. Once or twice he touched her thigh, warning her to stay on topic, and not start a political rant—one of her many failings. The hell with that! If ranting was what it took to have Milo touch her, then she'd set up her own soapbox next chance she got and climb right on board.

It must have gone on for an hour. The questions became repetitive, Jodie felt sleep deprivation catching up with her, and Milo finally interjected.

"My client has answered everything," he said. "You have no direct evidence linking her to Spectrum."

"Well, we—"

"If you did, you would have thrown it into the ring by now."

"She was there, with those people."

"No law against that," Milo replied. "She's also very high profile, and I don't think our American cousins will take kindly to your arresting one of their own on such flimsy evidence."

"We don't let things like that influence us."

"Well you should. Someone in this station leaked her name to the press." Jodie's head shot up. This was news to her. "I had to run the gauntlet of press photographers to get in here today."

"We don't care who her daddy is," one of the detectives sneered. "She gets treated the same as all the rest."

"Wouldn't have it any other way," Milo shot back. "But you've asked your questions, she's answered them, so what happens now? You don't have enough to charge her—"

"Yet. Our enquiry isn't complete."

"You don't have enough to charge her, and have no grounds to apply for an extension."

"Our forty-eight hours aren't up yet."

"You can hold her for another night, if it makes you feel better, but you and I both know she has nothing of value to give you." Milo glowered at the hapless pair. "You're pissing in the wind, gentlemen."

The verbal sparring went on for a while. Jodie said nothing, watching Milo's lovely mouth, fascinated by the way his sculpted lips moved when he spoke, wondering how they would feel if he moved them the same way over her body.

"She's a flight risk," one of the detectives said. "She only has a rented flat in London, with no real ties to the community. She has a wealthy family on the other side of the pond who could easily arrange for her to be spirited out of the country."

"Her father hopes to be elected to the senate, so I can't see him doing that," Milo replied. "And she won't go back to her flat. I'll take responsibility for her."

He will?

Eventually the detectives agreed to release her on police bail.

"What does that mean?" Jodie asked.

"It means you won't be charged with anything—"

"What a relief. Thank you, Milo!"

"Don't thank me yet. They're still investigating, and if they come up with anything, then could still charge you."

She jutted her chin. "There's nothing for them to come up with."

"We'll see."

"Why won't you believe me?"

"It doesn't matter what I believe. It's what they can prove, or think they can, that matters."

"Oh."

"You will have to surrender your passport, report to the police every day, and not have anything to do with your fellow arrestees, or any other questionable groups for that matter."

"Okay, I get it. I have to lay low for a while. But why can't I go back to my flat?"

"You won't get a moment's peace. The press has got wind of this, and they'd hound you night and day. I don't think that would please Daddy."

"Fuck Daddy."

Her language, or perhaps her venom, clearly surprised him. He sent her a considering look, made no comment, but still didn't smile.

"Where shall I live then?"

"You can move in with Hal and me until this is over. We have a spare room."

"You guys live together." Shit, she hadn't pegged him as being gay. "Won't I be in the way?"

"We don't live together in the manner you seem to think," he replied caustically. "Come on, there will be papers to sign, then we'll get you out of here."

"Where's Hal?"

"Bringing the car around the back, so we can avoid the press."

"Oh, but I'd like to—"

"Haven't you been listening to a word I've said?" His sigh was loud and prolonged. "You say nothing to the press, absolutely nothing. If you do, I walk. Are we clear?"

"Yes, sir."

His lips actually twitched at that one. It wasn't a smile exactly, but it was a start.

"That would be *sir* with a capital S," he replied mildly.

"What!"

Ten minutes later, Jodie's purse had been returned to her. She checked the contents and found everything was there. Milo cast a professional eye over the papers she was asked to sign, and the conditions under which they were prepared to grant her bail. She signed when he told her she could.

"Okay," he said, taking her elbow. "Let's get the hell out of here. Always a pleasure, gentlemen," he added over his shoulder to the hovering detectives who stood, arms crossed, scowling at them.

"I'll need some clothes from my place," she said, sliding into the backseat of a shiny new Range Rover with Hal behind the wheel. "I feel dirty, and…well, like I spent the night in a cell."

"Give me your flat keys," Milo replied, getting into the passenger seat. "Hal will drop us home, then go on to yours and pick up the things you'll need."

"How will you know what I need, Hal?"

His deep, rich laugher echoed around the cabin of the car. "What's the matter, babe? Don't you like surprises?"

Hal's amusement was infectious and she found herself laughing as well. "Okay then, hot shot, do your worst."

As she passed the keys through the gap in the front seats she caught Milo's glance lingering on her wrist.

"Glad it healed okay," he said.

Hell, he remembered her! Jodie gasped when he looked back at her and sent her an exaggerated wink, accompanied by a heated smile that went straight to her pussy.

Chapter Four

"Okay, Hal," Milo said when his buddy stopped the car outside their Battersea apartment building. "Make sure you check Jodie's place out thoroughly."

"You want me to leave anything I find where it is?"

"Of course."

"What are you guys talking about?" Jodie asked as Milo opened the car door for her. "What do you expect to find?"

Hal waved and drove off, leaving Milo alone with Jodie. He was annoyed with himself for winking at her, unsure what impulse had made him do it. Despite the fact that his cock had taken a shine to her, Ms. Bisset needed to be kept at arm's length. She spelled the sort of trouble Milo could definitely do without. He pressed the code to open the main front door to the building, and ushered Jodie into the spacious foyer ahead of him.

"Wow!" He stood behind her, watching as she rotated her head, trying to take it all in. "This is quite some place."

Milo tried to see the marble foyer through her eyes. All the mirrors, plants, and discreet art on the walls had impressed him, too, first time he'd seen it. There was an arrangement of soft furniture and low tables to one side, where visitors could wait, but no doorman. Instead the place was protected by state-of-the-art security devices, some of which Milo and Hal had installed themselves and the other residents knew nothing about.

"This used to be a warehouse," he replied, leading her toward the elevator. "It was redeveloped for housing some years ago. I happened to be in the right place at the right time, and picked up the penthouse at rock-bottom price. Battersea wasn't a safe area then, so it was a bit of a gamble that just happened to pay off."

"I'll bet it did."

Milo placed his key in the slot that would take the elevator direct to the penthouse. He only discovered when it was too late to do anything about it that being alone with Jodie in such a confined space was another bad idea. He'd been trying to ignore his growing attraction toward her by reminding himself of her foolish ideology. It wasn't working. Something stronger than his own will deprived him of the ability to hold that thought. She looked up at him, her lips shiny and moist, just as the elevator jerked into motion and their hands touched. Her eyes widened, as though she too felt an electric charge had passed between them. Shit, this was *so* going to end badly!

"You didn't answer my question," she said in a soft, throaty voice. "What must Hal leave where it is?"

Before he could respond, the elevator reached its destination and the doors slid smoothly open, directly into Milo's open-plan loft.

"Wow!" Jodie said for a second time. "This is awesome."

"Glad you like it."

"What's not to like? Especially that view." She stood by the full-length windows that looked directly over the Thames. A barge slowly made its way up the river, belching smoke. A pleasure craft came the opposite way, two bikini-clad women sprawled over the foredeck, making the most of the hot weather. "This place is huge," she said, turning in a full circle, taking in the bleached-oak furniture, the open-plan kitchen, and the dining table that could comfortably seat a dozen.

"I'll give you the guided tour in a moment. But first, to answer your question, Hal will check your bedsit for listening devices."

Her expression was incredulous, all wide eyes and slack mouth. "You've got to be kidding me."

"Afraid not." He removed his jacket and threw it across a chair. "Think about it. If this *was* a setup, then the people who did it will want to keep tabs on you. Speaking of which, turn your cell phone off."

"Why?"

"Your location can be traced all the time it's switched on."

Jodie reached into her bag, found her phone, and made a big deal out of switching it off. "I think you've watched too many spy movies."

"Don't you ever do as you're told?"

"I have a questioning mind." She shrugged. "Not my fault. Anyway, I think you're way overreacting."

"Am I?" He shot her a look. "It isn't me that just got arrested."

"Okay, point made. But how will anyone reach me if my phone's off?"

"Who are you expecting to hear from? Your family knows to call me, and you're not allowed to contact any of your radical friends."

"They are *not* radicals!"

"Whatever. You can use the landline here if you need to make calls, but make sure you suppress the number, and don't give it out or tell anyone where you are."

"Why do you suppose I was the target...if I was?" she asked.

"Why do you?"

She shook her head. "I don't necessarily." She paced up and down the large loft, clearly trying to articulate her thoughts. "It's just that my dad—well, let's just say even control freaks feel intimidated by him."

"But he can't control you?"

"Right, and it drives him crazy. Still, it's not my intention to derail his career."

"All I can tell you is the press knew all about your arrest before we even arrived to save your cute arse. If they knew, Daddy must know but, far as I can tell, he's made no attempt to contact you, or to get you out."

"True." She looked momentarily upset, but quickly recovered. "But don't forget the time difference."

"Jodie, your dad is a career diplomat. He could have set wheels in motion without leaving the comfort of his own bed."

"Yeah, and he probably has. He'll know by now exactly what happened and will be covering his ass. The last thing he wants is for his delinquent daughter to mess up his political ambitions."

"You really hate him, don't you?" Milo leaned against the breakfast bar and crossed his arms over his chest, curious about the depth of her animosity. "Mind you, if his first thought is for himself, I can't say that I blame you."

"Hate is a strong word." She canted her head, as though reassessing her feelings. "You want my take on what he'll be doing now?"

Milo nodded. "That would be useful."

"He'll be setting his publicity people to spin the incident to his advantage. A daughter who cares about the underprivileged, isn't afraid to voice her opinions and stand up for what she believes in, how proud he is of me because of it, blah de blah…" Jodie wrinkled her freckled nose. "The reverse is true, of course. He hates that I have *causes*. His attitude makes me sick to the stomach."

"Right, with good reason, I guess." Milo levered his body away from the counter. "We'll talk properly later, but right now I'm guessing you're beat, and hungry, too. So am I. Let's get some brunch going, then I'll show you your room. You can shower, get some rest, and later the three of us can have a brain-storming session about your situation."

"Sounds like a plan." Jodie stifled a yawn with the back of her hand, bone weary now she was out of jail and, temporarily at least, free to live her life. "I'll cook breakfast."

"Nah, leave it to me. I know where everything is."

"You sure? I don't mind pulling my weight."

Before he could respond, Milo's cell phone rang. "It's overseas," he said, checking the display. "Probably your brother. Irrationally, Milo really wanted it to be her old man, phoning because he cared, rather than to tear her a new one. He wasn't holding his breath. "Hanson," he said, answering the call. "Hey, Paul, how you doing? Yeah, she's out, and she's right here. Want to speak with her?"

"What happened?" Paul asked. "Can you tell me anything before I speak with Jodie? Is she all right?"

"She's shaken, but basically fine. As to what happened, too early to say." He gave Paul a brief rundown on the police findings.

"Who would have given them the tip-off?" Paul asked.

"Good question." And one that Milo had been asking himself. "All I know is, the press was onto it, but we managed to keep Jodie away from them."

"Shit! How did they get to hear so fast?"

"You know how the grapevine works."

A sigh echoed down the line. "Yeah, the old man had already heard, before I could tell him myself. He's spitting tacks."

"Didn't try to contact his daughter, though," Milo said before he could stop himself.

"He got right on to me, and we thought it best to wait until we heard from you."

For *we* Milo read *he* as in Bisset Senior, would-be senator and manipulator extraordinaire.

"Presumably the American embassy didn't get involved for the same reason."

"Right. They're on standby, in case Jodie needs them."

A bit late for that. "Well, there's not much more I can tell you right now. We're looking into the people Jodie mixed with, see what shakes loose. Someone must know something. Someone always does. I'll keep you informed."

"Thanks, Milo. I owe you one."

Milo glanced at Jodie, who was watching him intently as she listened to his end of the conversation. Paul had just confirmed their father was calling the shots from his end, confirming Jodie's prediction that his first thought would be damage limitation. That knowledge ignited Milo's anger, and increased his determination to look out for Jodie. Someone had to.

"Here, your sister needs a word," was all he could trust himself to say.

Milo passed his cell phone to Jodie and gave her some privacy by taking himself off into the kitchen. He rummaged in the fridge for the ingredients for a massive fry-up. If ever a situation called for comfort food, this was it. *Fuck healthy eating*!

"Thanks," Jodie said, sliding onto a stool at the counter and passing Milo his phone back. "I think I've stopped Paul from panicking about me."

"Here," he said, passing her silverware, napkins, and place mats. "Make yourself useful."

She set out the mats on the counter, adding water glasses and condiments as Milo passed them to her. She worked efficiently, and in silence. He liked that about her. Women had a tendency to talk, just for the sake of it, but Jodie didn't seem to care if she appeared anti-social.

"Help yourself to juice," he said, handing her a carton.

"Thanks." She poured them both a glass and downed half of hers in one hit. "Ah, that's better. I was parched."

"Want some coffee? It's already made."

"Thanks."

Milo handed her a steaming mug just as the lift doors swished open and Hal appeared, carrying a heavy bag.

"Ah, breakfast. Good. I'm famished." He smiled at Jodie. "Here's your stuff, hon. Hope I didn't forget anything."

"It looks like you brought the entire contents of my wardrobe. I tend to travel light."

"Yeah, I noticed that."

"Any unwelcome guests been to Jodie's apartment?" Milo asked, turning around from the stove where he was frying bacon.

"No, nothing I could find."

That was good enough for Milo. If there was something to find, Hal would have found it.

"It'll be a few minutes yet," Milo said. "Show Jodie her room, Hal, and give her a moment to stash her stuff."

"Yes, boss." Hal saluted Milo, smiled at Jodie, and took her hand. "This way, ma'am," he said.

* * * *

Jodie was woken by sunshine bathing her face. She stretched, enjoying the feel of the crisp cotton sheets that cocooned her, unable at first to remember where she was. Certainly not in her own crappy apartment, that was for sure. She didn't run to Egyptian cotton. Besides, the windows at her place were too small to let in so much sunshine.

It came back to her in a heated rush, spoiling her soporific state when she recalled the shock and absolute horror of being arrested. The humiliation of being treated like a criminal—worse, a criminal suspected of working against the interests of the West—burned through her like acid. She leaned up on one elbow and shook her head. How had this happened to her? Damn it, she'd never had so much as a speeding ticket in her entire life, and now this.

Feeling sorry for herself would do no good. All that mattered was clearing her name—for her own sake, rather than that of her family. What mattered almost as much was getting Milo to believe in her innocence. She had thought his intransigent stance was thawing after they left the police station, and later when he spoke up for her to her brother.

It seemed she was mistaken. He had cooked the three of them an enormous brunch—doing it with the same efficiency and attention to detail she suspected he devoted to everything he did. Hal kept the conversation rolling while they ate, but Milo didn't address a single word directly to her. She caught him looking at her intently on several occasions, frowning as though he couldn't quite decide what to make of her, but it was obvious he somehow blamed her for the position she had found herself in.

Well, Mr. Perfect, I'll just have to find a way to show you you're wrong about that. She was as stubborn as her father was when it came to getting what she wanted—but, thank God, nowhere near so selfish and self-centered. Still, at least some of her dad's implacability had rubbed off on her. She was now on a mission to prove herself to the man she hadn't been able to stop fantasizing about for more than ten years.

There was a huge bathroom that went with the guys' guest room. Once she had eaten, Jodie stood in the shower for a long time, washing the smell of jail desperation off her skin and hair. Then she'd fallen into bed, her hair still wet, and slept soundly for…for how long? She glanced at the bedside clock and gasped. It was six in the evening. She'd slept for five hours straight.

She slid out of bed, used the facilities, then glanced in the mirror and expelled a second gasp. She really should have dried her hair before sleeping. Unsurprisingly, it now resembled a haystack. With a wry sigh, she dragged a brush through it, pulling the wild curls back from her face and securing them in place with a clip she found in her purse. She blushed as she rummaged for underwear in the drawer where she'd placed it, strangely excited to think that Hal's hands had touched it as he packed it all for her. Shame he wasn't in the room to help her into it—although she suspected he and Milo would both be more efficient at removing a woman's lingerie.

Get a grip, girl. She really should not be lusting after her temporary hosts, especially since one of them obviously didn't like her very much. Besides, Jodie was very selective when it came to men. She didn't often get the hots for a guy—now she appeared to be fantasizing about two at once. She'd had a girlfriend at college who was into that scene in a big way, and described in graphic detail what she and her Master got up to. It had both shocked and excited Jodie to hear all the salacious details of beatings, punishments, bondage, and the most excruciating-sounding implements of torture her friend embraced. She wondered what it would be like to use pain as a means of achieving gratification, but couldn't imagine ever being in a position to find out.

Jodie chose a pretty girly-pink bra and matching panties, for no other reason than they made her feel feminine. After her ordeal of earlier, she badly needed a shot of confidence. She pulled on a pair of loose pants and a sleeveless top, and thrust her feet into low-heeled mules.

"Okay," she said to her reflection, deciding that facial cosmetics would make it seem as though she was trying to make an impression. "Let the fight back begin."

Her room was at the end of a corridor that led off from the main area in the loft. There were closed doors on either side of it— presumably the guys' rooms—and an open archway to a large office with two workstations. She found both men in there, heads bent over computers.

"Ah, there is life after death." Hal grinned as his gaze slid slowly down the length of her. "Feeling better? You sure as hell look it."

"Much. Sorry I slept for so long. I didn't think I'd be able to, what with all the stuff churning away inside my head, but it seems I was wrong."

"No problem." Milo glanced up at her, but didn't show any reaction to her improved appearance. "You clearly needed it. Come on, we'll be more comfortable in the other room."

Both men, she noticed, closed their browsers and shut down their computers before leaving their desks. Presumably they didn't want her to see what they had been doing. Like she would look!

"It's a nice evening," Hal said, opening the doors to a large terrace that overlooked the river. "Let's sit out here and have a glass of wine."

He left again, presumably in search of said wine, and Jodie was alone with Milo. Without Hal to break the silence, Jodie felt the same brittle tension spring up between them again, but couldn't think of a single thing to say to relieve it. Milo wasn't looking at her so she took the opportunity to check him out. He'd changed out of his fancy clothes, into jeans that hugged his ass and a plain T-shirt. With his hair falling across his forehead, he looked just as good as he had in his bespoke suit—good enough to devour whole. Her entire body ached—not just for him, but for his approval. Why it should matter to her so much, she couldn't have said. It was just the way it was.

Jodie felt honey trickling from her cunt as she continued to observe him, and wondered why life was so damned unfair. She had no shortage of offers from guys who wanted to get to know her better. None of them rocked her world. Instead she was fixated on a guy who not only disliked her, but disapproved of everything she stood for.

"Take a seat," Milo said, indicating one of the overstuffed sofas. The bastard looked faintly amused, presumably because he'd been watching her fighting against the impulse to rip his clothes off and lick every inch of his body. She tossed her head and dutifully sat, deciding that if the arrogant jerk ever did put a move on her, she'd tell him to take a hike. *Yeah, like that's gonna happen!*

Milo sat across from her and arranged his long, muscular legs casually in front of him, crossing them at the ankles and leaning his elbow on the arm of the sofa. A deeply disturbing jolt rocked her as he focused intelligent gray eyes on her face, as though he could see directly into her soul. Unable to stand the unnerving stillness for a second longer, she finally spoke.

"Did you manage to get some rest, too?" she asked.

His brows shot up. "Excuse me?"

"You said in the police station that you'd only had two hours' sleep. You look rested, so I assumed—"

"Don't worry about it. Hal and I are used to getting by without much sleep."

"Through your military training?"

"Yeah, you could say."

But saying anything didn't appear to figure high on his agenda, and once again they submerged into a simmering silence. Well, that was it. She'd tried. If he wanted to just sit there, sending her probing, disapproving glances, then he could knock himself out. She could take it.

She absolutely could.

She focused her gaze on the river, watching the activity. There always appeared to be something going on. Craft of all shapes and sizes drifted past, loud party music floating up from some of them. How nice it must be, Jodie thought, to have nothing more taxing on one's mind than having a good time. When was the last time she had been in that position? She really couldn't remember.

Hal joined them, clutching an open bottle, and the loaded tension evaporated.

"White wine okay with you, babe?" he asked.

"Sure, thanks."

She would have been surprised if they'd opted for white wine, too. It wasn't a very masculine drink, and one thing she could say about these two with absolute certainty was they were one hundred percent thoroughbred, pure virile male. Sure enough, Hal reached into a cooler, flipped the tops off two bottles of beer, and handed one to Milo.

"Thanks, mate," he said.

"What happens now?" Jodie asked after they had sat in silence for what seemed like forever, sipping their drinks, Milo still avoiding eye contact with her.

"About your situation?" Milo asked.

"Of course. I can't stay here indefinitely, so we need to figure out what's going on."

"You can stay as long as you like, darling," Hal said, blowing her a kiss.

Jodie laughed in spite of herself. "I'd only cramp your style."

"We've been doing some work on your case this afternoon," Milo said. "We've amassed quite a bit of information about your Camden Town pals."

"Oh really." He clearly didn't like what he'd found, but his scathing tone irritated Jodie. "Do share."

"Did you know that your friend Jeff has a criminal record?"

Jodie put her glass aside and sat bolt upright. "No. What for?"

"Breaking and entering, criminal damage—"

"Jeff is a thief?" She shook her head. "I don't believe it."

"He didn't steal anything," Hal said. "He broke into a lab where they keep animals for medical experiments and tried to release them."

"Ah, that's different."

She expected Milo to make a derisive comment. He didn't. "I like animals, too," he surprised her by saying. "But I'm not sure that's the right way to go about saving them from all that shit."

Jodie was affronted by his superior tone. "Oh, and I suppose you know a better way."

She didn't realize she'd thrust her chest out until she noticed that both of them had fixed steady gazes on her tits. She blushed, annoyed with herself because a tiny part of her was pleased to have gotten their attention, albeit by use of underhand tactics. "Sometimes the direct approach is the only way," she said, picking up her glass and taking another long swig.

"I couldn't agree more," Hal said, his gaze still glued to her chest.

"How did you find that out about Jeff, anyway?" she asked. "Police records aren't in the public domain in this country."

"We have our ways."

Milo stretched both arms above his head and yawned. His shirt rode up, giving Jodie an up-close view of a toned midriff covered with a light dusting of dark, curling chest hair. It ran in a line down the center of his belly and disappeared beneath the waistband of his jeans. What she would give to trace it to its source—with her tongue.

"We hack into the criminal records computer," Hal said, laughing.

Her eyes flew wide. "You don't!"

Hal shrugged. "How else are we supposed to know what's going on?"

"What if you get caught?"

"We won't," Milo said.

She recalled them both hitting various keys before they shut down their computers. Well, far be it from her to tell them how to behave. They were clearly very bad boys who played by their own rules. Jodie moistened her lips. Now why did she find that prospect so appealing?

"We also found out that your friends Phil and Betty spent six months in a remote part of Pakistan a few years ago," Milo told her. "The part of Pakistan that has training camps for a certain terrorist organization that shall remain nameless."

"I knew they'd been there," Jodie replied pensively. "They don't make any secret out of it. They were on retreat."

Milo curled his upper lip. "Sure they were."

"Are you always so cynical?" she asked.

Milo shrugged impossibly broad shoulders. "In my line of work I don't come across too many situations where cynicism doesn't fit the bill."

"He saves the sarcasm for people," Hal said, grinning.

Jodie treated Milo to a withering glance, to which he showed no reaction. Infuriated, she addressed her next comment to Hal.

"Accounting for his vast and continuing popularity, no doubt," she said.

"Just so that you know," Milo said. "I don't give a flying fuck what people think of me. I am what I am. Get over it."

"Yes, I got that part."

"Children, children!" Hal waved a placating hand between them. Only then did Jodie realize that she and Milo were leaning toward one another, mere inches separating their faces. How had that happened? "Play nice or you're both in detention."

Milo leaned back in his chair, and took a long slug from his beer, saying nothing.

"Sorry," Jodie said, recalling she was a guest in their home. Besides, one of them needed to act like a grownup. "I guess I'm still on edge."

"Well, anyway, about your friends. It explains why they were on the police radar," Hal said.

"I suppose so. I don't think they were aware of it, though."

"It also explains why the Camden Town house was under surveillance," Hal continued. "No one goes to Pakistan to *find* themselves."

Jodie opened her mouth to argue, then shut it again. He was probably right.

"I've been thinking about this whole business of us being arrested," Jodie said. "It's a bit convenient, don't you think, the police finding plans for a firebombing lying about in plain sight." She noticed the two guys share a glance, but neither one of them interrupted her. "Surely something that sensitive wouldn't be committed to paper at all."

"The same thought had occurred to us," Milo admitted. "The way the police told it, the papers were on the coffee table in the lounge when the raid went down, as though you'd been discussing it."

Jodie shook her head. "I already explained, that house is always full of people coming and going. Anyone could have left the papers there days ago and no one would be any the wiser. Keeping house isn't high on their agenda."

Milo fixed her with a penetrating gaze. "So your fingerprints won't be found on them?"

"No, of course not. I already told you…Oh shit!" Jodie's hand flew to her mouth. "I picked a load of things up and moved them out the way yesterday, so we had space for our coffee cups."

Chapter Five

Milo watched the color drain from Jodie's face. Her eyes had taken on a wild sheen and an expression of absolute horror filtered across her lovely features. If he'd doubted her innocence before now, her reaction would have put him straight. She was guilty of nothing more sinister than good intentions and a lousy choice in friends. Cynic that he was, Milo knew all too well where they could land a person. It was all he could do not to stand up, pull Jodie into his arms, and comfort her in the way that sprang spontaneously to mind—and to other parts of his anatomy.

Professionalism won out over his raging lust. Just.

"Don't worry," he contented himself with saying. "If your prints are on the papers, we can make a good argument for them having got there innocently."

She sent him a glance loaded with trepidation. "Yes, but it doesn't look too good for me, does it?"

"We'll start fighting back first thing in the morning." Hal reached across to touch her hand. "Fight fire with fire, that's always been our motto. We don't do passive."

"By delving into the background of my friends, trying to put the blame on them?"

"You can bet your life they'll be doing the same thing to you," Milo said, the sympathy he'd felt for her fading, even if he did reluctantly admire her loyalty. "Besides, if there's nothing to find, we can't harm them."

"I suppose." She plucked restlessly at the arm of the couch, frowning. "Still, it seems…well, I don't know, dirty, somehow."

"Terrorism's a dirty business," Milo replied.

"And finding ways to prove you had an innocent reason to touch those papers, if you did touch them, is called creating reasonable doubt," Hal added.

"But even if you get me off, there will still be a suspicion hanging over me. I'll be on every watch list on both sides of the pond."

"No good deed ever goes unpunished," Milo told her, reaching behind him for another beer.

"I guess not." Jodie shook her head. "Perhaps I've been too trusting."

Milo frowned. "The way I see it, either one of your buddies really is up to his or her neck in this shit, got careless, and really did leave those papers on the table, or—"

"Or," Hal finished for him, serious for once, "someone's deliberately targeting you in order to get to your dad. Any idea who that might be?"

Jodie harrumphed. "How long have you got? He's a politician. He makes enemies. That's what politicians do best."

"Cynicism at last," Milo said with the ghost of a smile. "Ata girl!"

"Your attitude is obviously rubbing off on me."

"It might be an idea to speak to Paul about your dad's enemies," Hal suggested. "See if he has any ideas. Might as well work both angles at once."

"Good thinking." Milo crossed one foot across his opposite thigh and leaned his elbow on his raised knee. "My money's on the political angle."

"I remember you being in the States years ago," Jodie said to Milo. "You, Paul, Raoul, and Zeke and a couple of other guys hung out at Dad's place for a long weekend."

"And you crashed out of a tree on top of our heads," Milo reminded her.

Hal laughed. "I'd have paid good money to see that. American and British joint elite forces crushed by a falling teenager."

"I wasn't quite into my teens at the time," Jodie replied, laughing. "I was trying to get close enough to hear what you were all saying. I figured it had to do with girls, because Paul kept shooing me away when I tried to listen. Well, I wasn't having that. I absolutely had to know what happened between the sexes. Not my fault," she continued, shrugging. "Like I said before, I was born with an innate sense of curiosity. I like to know how things work, and the more someone told me I was too young, the more determined I became to find out."

Hal sent her a smoldering look. "If you need any reminders."

Milo concentrated his gaze on Jodie, wondering if she knew how adorable she looked when the devil got into her, as it had at that moment. Her eyes had lost their haunted look as she exchanged banter with Hal, giving as good as she got. Shit, but he wanted her bad! He didn't have to ask Hal to know he felt the same way. It was a while since they'd found a woman they both wanted to share. Now they had one, living under their own roof, and Milo was supposed to keep his hands off her. Geez!

Just for a moment, he allowed his mind to drift in that direction, wondering if she'd go for it. *Get over yourself. You can't have her, and that's an end to it. Face it, you don't even like her very much.*

"We need sustenance," Milo said.

"I'll go out for Chinese," Hal said, standing. "I assume you like Chinese, babe?"

"Sure, but can't you phone out for it?"

"We could, but we prefer to collect it ourselves. Call us paranoid, but we prefer not to have strangers seeing this place, not even delivery kids."

"Oh, I see."

"Anything you don't like?"

"No, surprise me."

"Behave yourselves while I'm gone," Hal said, wagging a finger at each of them in turn. "Don't forget, you're still on detention watch, the pair of you."

Milo shot him the finger. "You're full of it."

The moment Hal disappeared into the elevator Milo became conscious of a tension that hadn't been there when his pal had been around to drive the conversation. He glanced at Jodie, who looked so different to the way she had in the police station. She had washed her hair and it now tumbled down her back, thick and shiny, defying any efforts she might have made to instill some sort of order into it. Milo was glad. He liked it just the way it was. He liked brunettes. Damn it, he liked her, despite her warped ideas about social justice and the ways to go about achieving it.

She kept sending him sideways glances, as though she could sense the tension as well. Did she know it was sexual tension? Shit, *he* should have been the one to go for food. It was a seriously bad idea to remain here alone with her.

Since leaving the SAS three years previously, Milo had found it hard to settle to anything. So, too, had Hal. They missed the action and camaraderie, but not the bureaucracy and political in-fighting that hampered everything the squad was required to do. He and Hal had run through a string of women since getting out, but none of them had held their attention for long. The thought of being tied down when they were both free spirits at heart had made sure of that.

But there was something about Jodie that was different. He could look at her and not experience his usual commitment phobia. He found that deeply disturbing, because he *definitely didn't like her* or her campaigns. She was looking at him, probably unaware there was an age-old question in her eyes. In an effort to disabuse her of any ideas she might have picked up from the charged atmosphere, he spoke with a deliberate edge of indifference in his voice.

"Being arrested isn't exactly a walk in the park," he said. "Perhaps the experience will make you choose your causes more carefully in future."

Jodie glared at him like she couldn't believe her ears. She cursed beneath her breath and leapt to her feet, sloshing wine over her hand in her haste to put her glass aside.

"Of all the arrogant, high-handed, patronizing…what gives you the damned right to lecture me?" She shook a fist of him. "What precisely have I done that you find so offensive? Do tell." He opened his mouth to tell her, but she didn't give him the chance. "I didn't ask to come here, you invited me. But my presence clearly offends. If you're just planning to look down at me all the time, and denigrate the things I believe in, then I'll make alternative arrangements."

Her reaction stunned him, partly because she was right. He *had* overreacted and now found himself on the back foot. "Honest truth?" he asked.

"That would be refreshing," she replied caustically, resuming her seat with apparent reluctance.

"Okay, here's the way I see it. You had a tough time of it as a kid, being dragged all over the globe by an ambitious father. I get that part, really I do, but a lot of other kids have a much harder time of it, and don't grow up with massive chips on their shoulders. I'm betting you never went hungry, or without the latest *must-have* gadget, or without the best education money could buy. I'm betting you were never abused, or exposed to the seedier side of life that a lot of other kids have to endure."

"And your point is?" she demanded, her eyes shooting daggers at him.

"You pick your causes, telling yourself you believe in them, but all you really care about is getting back at Daddy dearest."

"Ah, so you don't think the Syrian refugees aren't worth bothering with? It's their mess, let them sort it out for themselves."

"I didn't say that, but there are better ways to go about it. The major charities are all in there, doing what they can through official channels."

"It's not enough."

"It's never enough, but it's the way the system works. If you carry on with your high-profile demonstrations, it will put more pressure on American and European countries to intercede."

"Duh, well that's kinda the point."

"You want our troops to go piling in, involve themselves in a fight that doesn't concern them?"

"Well, yes." But she sounded a little less certain of herself. "It will bring it to an end a lot quicker."

"Oh, honey." Milo shook his head, wondering if there was a time when he'd ever been that naïve. "Look at Iraq. Look at Egypt."

"It just doesn't seem right that all those innocent people—"

"Have you ever been to a war zone?"

"No, and I've never been to a famine-hit country either, but I know they exist."

Milo didn't know where to start with her. His bedroom was the most appealing option, but that wasn't going to happen. "I hate the system as much as you do, but sometimes it's better not to tinker."

"Just bury your head, and pretend all these atrocities don't occur?" She sent him a scathing look. "Get on with our privileged lives here in the West and forget all the heartache and suffering that goes on elsewhere?"

"Don't use world politics to get back at your old man," Milo shot at her.

Jodie jumped to her feet again, pushing her face close to his. "You might think you know all there is to know about wars, but you know nothing about me, so don't be so quick to judge."

"Then tell me," Milo replied, his words intended as a stark challenge. "Help me to understand what landed you in jail today."

She moved away and stood with her back to him, staring out at the river, but probably not seeing it. "Paul's fifteen years older than me," she said, so quietly that Milo had to strain his ears to hear her. "I was definitely a mistake," she added bitterly, "and an inconvenience. I was never made to feel any other way. By the time I was old enough to realize I had a brother, he was away at college, back in the States. Dad had his career all mapped out for him. He would go into the military, and naturally he would excel."

"I thought you got along with your brother."

"Oh, I do. But he's more a friend than a brother. Dad's proud of him, because he did as he was told and became one of the youngest colonels in the US Army. That looks great on Dad's resume," she added bitterly.

"And what did he have planned for you?"

"Oh, an Ivy League college, a *suitable* career, and then an even more *suitable* marriage to a man he approved of, and who would have been of use to him. Hell, he probably had him already picked out."

Milo's contemptuous stance softened. "But you rebelled, and wrecked it all."

"Yep." She turned to face him. "I'm the first person I know of who's ever stood up to him and come out on the winning side."

Hmm, Milo had met men like that before. They hated to be beaten, which made him wonder if he really had given up on Jodie. He certainly wasn't in any big rush to contact her and make sure she was okay. That said a lot.

"That must have taken courage."

She shrugged. "I guess I'm too much like him in some respects. I don't like anyone telling me what to do, or how to live my life."

"You're not good at taking orders?" There went Milo's fledgling hopes of getting her to play with him and Hal. Not that it had been a serious consideration, had it?

Jodie emitted a hollow laugh. "Depends what I'm being ordered to do, and whether I want to do it."

"Sounds like a challenge." *And I bet I can make you want to. I'll just love seeing you begging on bended knees to be fucked.* "Presumably your father has finally seen the light, and knows he can't control you."

"Hardly. He's still at me to return home."

"Why?"

"To stand at his side and help him with his campaign, of course. He wants to show himself as the down-to-earth, patriotic family man with his colonel son on one side, and his obedient little daughter on the other."

Milo frowned. "What about your mother? You haven't mentioned her at all in any of this."

"I was getting to her." She tossed her head, tears glistening in her lovely eyes. "Trust me, the story of my life just gets better and better." She met his gaze and held it. "My earliest memory of my mother is of her pouring vodka over her cornflakes at the breakfast table. Well, not literally, but you get the picture, I'm sure."

"Oh, shit!"

"That about covers it." Jodie crossed her arms around her torso and hugged herself. "Not that I blame her for her addiction. I guess it's about the only way she could cope with living with a control freak like Dad. He never would have given her a divorce, you see." Jodie blew air through her lips. "Far as he's concerned, Mom signed on for better or worse, and there's nothing more to be said."

"Who raised you then?"

"A series of nannies. I learned to be self-sufficient at a young age and made the best of my own company."

"Did your mom ever get help for her alcoholism?"

"Oh yeah, she's been into rehab so often they ought to name a wing of the Betty Ford clinic after her. She's probably paid for one. She comes out sober, but it never lasts. She manages to hide it well, but I don't think Dad wants to risk her being on the campaign trail too much. She copes pretty well in small social situations, in her own home, where she feels in control. She's from a good Southern family, and manners are second nature to her. You'd have to know her real well to realize she's totally wasted half the time. But when it comes to the realities of modern-day campaigning, I don't think Dad trusts her to stay sober enough to help him."

"Hence his need to have you back."

"Yeah well, my being arrested has blown that ambition to smithereens."

Milo sent her an assessing, sideways glance. "Sure you didn't make the arrangements for your arrest yourself?"

"Just a goddamned minute!"

She swirled to face him, tears leaking from eyes that radiated hostility. Milo had spoken flippantly, trying to lighten the mood. He definitely hadn't meant to upset her even more. Her expression—the loneliness and fear he could detect beneath her brash stance—was his undoing. In two strides he covered the distance between them and pulled her into his arms. Her body collided with his. Hard. His arms closed around her, and he felt her breath peppering his cheek as she let out a startled little oath.

"I didn't mean to upset you, darling," he said softly. "That was a poor attempt at a joke."

"Your sense of humor needs some work."

He brushed escaped strands of hair away from her brow, along with a couple of errant tears that had slid down her cheek. "So I've been told."

"Okay, you can let me go now." But she didn't try to struggle free.

"Not a chance."

"But you don't like me."

"I might have been a tad hasty there."

She blinked up at him. "Did I hear you right? Was that an apology?"

"I jumped to conclusions without having all the facts. Hal will tell you I don't usually do that."

She was still looking up at him, her eyes now smoldering with a luminescence that hinted at a deeply passionate nature. "Then why this time?"

"I wish I knew. There's just something about you that brings out the worst in me. Still, there's one thing I'm absolutely sure about."

Her breathing hitched. "What's that?"

"If I don't kiss you, I'm gonna go out of my frigging mind."

When Jodie opened her mouth to gasp—whether in protest or acquiescence, Milo couldn't have said—he seized the opportunity to cover her lips with his, invading her conveniently open mouth with his tongue. A mewling sound slipped past their fused lips as Milo tightened his arms around her and deepened the kiss, causing longing, and raw carnality to heat his blood. His rigid cock painfully tested his zipper as it pressed into her belly. His hands drifted to her arse, pulling her harder against his erection. She kissed him right back, somehow still moaning and mewling as their passions ignited and any lingering doubts about the wisdom of his actions fled Milo's brain.

"Well, well," said an amused voice behind them. "When I said play nice, I wasn't sure this is quite what I had in mind."

Chapter Six

Jodie felt a white-hot rush of anticipation consume her. Every nerve ending in her body sprang enthusiastically to life as she lived through yet another erotic dream of Milo. This one was more realistic that usual. She could actually feel his lips, firm and demanding, fusing with her own. She savored the taste of his tongue as it explored her mouth with a lazy expertise that left her quivering with need. And no one would convince her that his capable hands weren't actually roaming over her body, making her cry out with need as he agitated her passions, and caused burning liquid heat to course through her veins.

If she opened her eyes she would wake up, aroused, frustrated, and alone in her own bed— again. And so she kept them firmly closed, and lived the dream for just a little longer.

The sound of a voice and a responding deep, rich masculine chuckle caught her off guard. That had never happened before. Milo's voice has never been so real in her dreams. And the tight arms pinning her against a rock-solid body, the feel of an impressive erection drilling against her belly, was too authentic to be a figment of the highly active imagination that had spent ten years fine-tuning her Milo fantasies.

She cautiously opened one eye and found herself gazing into Milo's sparkling gray eyes.

Holy shit, this was for real!

He *had* actually kissed her, and he'd done it because *he* wanted to. It was surreal. If Hal hadn't come back when he had, who knows where it would have led. Where it still might lead, if she had any say in the matter. Milo didn't seem bothered by Hal's appearance, and continued to hold Jodie very close. And then he did what she had never thought to see. He offered her a full-wattage, non-contrived, one-hundred-percent exceedingly wicked smile. It lit up his rugged features, emphasizing the fine lines around his eyes—eyes that glowed with hot intentions—and kissed the end of her nose.

"Your timing sucks, mate," he said to Hal, finally letting her go.

"You want me to go out and come back in again?"

"Yeah, in about two hours' time."

"Fuck you, I wanna play, too."

"Pardon?" Jodie, still dazed, must have misheard him. "What did you say?"

"He didn't say anything, darling." Milo shot Hal what appeared to be a warning glare. "He's talking out of his arse as usual."

Jodie would never tire of hearing a Brit say the word *arse*. It sounded glamorous and erotic, especially coming from the mouth of someone with such a polished, upper-class accent as Milo. She had no idea where he'd gone to school, but was willing to bet his education had taken place at one of England's more elite establishments. It showed.

"Let me help you with the food, Hal," Jodie said, moving into the kitchen, surprised her legs had the strength to support her, given the carnage Milo's kiss had done to her equilibrium.

To her astonishment, Hal slipped an arm around her waist and planted a gentle kiss on her lips.

"Why should he have all the fun?"

"Leave it, Hal," Milo said sharply.

He came into the kitchen as well, shooed Jodie out the way and decanted all the food into serving dishes. No eating straight from the foil containers in this establishment, obviously. Milo washed the containers in question under the tap, and then squashed them into the recycling bin. Clearly, he was housetrained. Gotta hand it to the military, she thought. The discipline never left its recruits.

They sat at the kitchen counter, Milo opened a bottle of red wine and poured for them all, and they started to eat. The atmosphere was charged again, pulsating with something Jodie couldn't put a name to. There was a lot of eye contact going on between Milo and Hal, and Jodie had no idea what that was all about. It was like they were communicating without the need for words. Jodie felt excluded, and found it exhausting trying to keep up with them.

"I'm curious about something," she said. "How come Paul knew to call you for help?"

"He didn't," Milo replied. "He called Raoul. Remember him?"

"How can I forget?" A giggle slipped past her guard. "It was his head I almost landed on when I fell from that tree."

"Right, well he runs a covert agency that helps out in certain situations."

Jodie widened her eyes. "Military operations?"

"Sometimes," Hal said evasively. "He has people all over the States, and in other countries, too. We've all served, and been frustrated by the red-tape bullshit you've probably come against when trying to help your refugees. By keeping below the radar, we can sometimes get things done without anyone being the wiser."

"Ah, now I understand the hacking into the criminal records thing. I wondered why you just happened to possess that skill."

"That's pretty basic stuff," Milo said. "We go other, way more sensitive places sometimes. Places where the establishment can't risk being caught poking their collective noses in." He leaned an elbow on the counter, totally at ease. To Jodie, he had never seemed more compelling. "It can be very informative."

"I'll just bet it can." Jodie suspected there was a great deal more to it than that, but also figured they probably would tell her. "I understand now why you weren't best pleased to be stuck with me. My problems must seem pretty insignificant compared to what you normally do."

"We're happy to help," Hal said, blowing her a kiss.

"What made Raoul start up his operation? I would have thought he'd be married with a couple of kids by now."

"He was married," Milo replied, his expression darkening. "To a Palestinian lady who helped the Americans and Israelis try to broker peace in her part of the world. She got killed in a stupid operation that never should have gone ahead. Raoul and Zeke got captured trying to save her. They were badly tortured—"

"That's so sad."

"Yeah well, now they run a horse farm in Wyoming, and control their agency from there," Hal said. "I don't think Raoul will ever know any peace until he avenges his wife's senseless death."

"Which means bringing down the US colonel who ordered the mission," Milo added. "And that would be tantamount to treason. No wonder the poor guy can't move on with his life."

Hal stood up and started stashing their empty plates in the dishwasher, waving aside her offer of help. When he returned to his seat, Jodie noticed another speaking look pass between the two men, and Milo give an imperceptible nod.

"Is there something you two aren't telling me?" she asked. "I get the feeling I'm being talked about behind my back."

"Only in a good way, babe," Hal assured her.

"Do share," she invited.

"There's no easy way to tell you this, and it will probably shock you." Milo took her hand and kissed the back of it, his tongue trailing lazily across her knuckles, setting her pulse racing. "And you have to understand from the outset that there's absolutely no pressure on you to agree."

"None whatsoever," Hal added, taking her other hand and mirroring Milo's actions.

Jodie's brain flooded with possibilities—none of them good. They had decided they couldn't help her after all. They both had significant others, who would return home any moment and demand to know what Jodie was doing there. No, they wouldn't be kissing her hands if that was the case.

Thinking of which, why was she letting Hal kiss her? Milo was the only man she'd ever wanted, and he appeared to be on the cusp of making a move on her. It wouldn't do to give the impression of being loose, and blow it. And yet Hal, with his blond surfer-boy looks, sparkling blue eyes, and infectious good humor, excited her passions just as much as Milo did. Wow, she hadn't seen that one coming. She shook her head in an effort to clear the fog whirling around inside it. Getting arrested must have put her through a character transplant.

"Just tell me," she said, glad they couldn't know that their combined attentions had caused her pussy to leak like a faulty faucet. Having two such gorgeous hunks plying her with attention did that to a girl, it seemed. "It can't be that bad."

"Depends if you really are averse to taking orders," Milo replied.

"Now you've definitely piqued my curiosity."

"We'd like to pique a hell of a lot more than that." Milo fixed her with a burning look. "Don't freak, but you need to understand that Hal and I are sexual Doms. You know what that means?"

You're what! "I think so. You like to order a woman about in the bedroom. Tie her up. Spank her. Make her do what you want."

"Sounds as though you've tried it," Hal said, squeezing the hand he was still holding.

"No, but I had a friend at college who was into it. She used to tell me things."

"Things that made you curious?" Milo asked.

"Well, I—"

Milo released her hand and lightly tapped her thigh. "Always say what you're thinking when we ask you a question, Jodie. Never prevaricate. Relationships like the one we're suggesting require complete honesty, and absolute trust."

"I haven't agreed to a relationship yet."

"No," Milo said, a slow, sexy smile illuminating his features. "You haven't, but you will."

His arrogance, his total belief in his ability to control her, both angered and excited Jodie. "You're very sure of yourself, Mr. Hanson."

"I've kissed you. I know how passionate you are. I'm also guessing you want to know more about our lifestyle. A lot more. Now, answer my question."

"Sir with a capital S," she muttered.

"Come again," Hal said.

"Sir with a capital S. That's what Milo said to me in the police station. Now it starts to make sense. And yes, I am curious, but I need to know what you would expect of me. Would I have to have sex with you both?"

"Absolutely," they replied in unison.

"Both at once?"

Milo nodded. "But not immediately. We'll train you, work up to that."

"I'm not good at pain."

"We'll get you used to that as well," Hal said. "And you'll take to it like a natural."

"How can you be so sure?"

"I thought you'd make an amazingly responsive sub as soon as I met you," Hal replied. "But someone who shall remain nameless never mixes business with pleasure, so I figured it wouldn't happen. When I got back with the food and saw what the two of you were doing, I couldn't quite believe it." *That makes two of us.* "You've broken thought his defenses, darling, and so the rules don't apply in your case. I'm glad, 'cause I gotta tell you, I want you pretty damned bad. Have done since first setting eyes on you."

Jodie gulped. "What, when I was in the police station, tired, dirty, and scared shitless?"

"And mouthing off," Milo added with a hint of a smile.

"Especially then," Hal said. "You looked so damned vulnerable, I just wanted to scoop you up and make it all go away for you."

Jodie was overcome. She somehow knew Hal hadn't said that just because he wanted to get laid. He wouldn't have any trouble finding female companionship if that's all it was. She could get used to being the object of their charm campaign, but reminded herself not to get carried away by their flattery. These guys were career philanderers. They were proposing a bit of fun while they sorted out her problems, that was all. Once that was done with, she would be history. Jodic didn't do casual flings with one guy at a time, much less two. But her body had other ideas. It was buzzing with expectation and she knew she wouldn't turn them down. It was time to broaden her horizons.

"About doing as I'm told." She shared a wry smile between them. "I'm not too good at that. I've been a rebel all my life, and that won't change. If I agree to do this, then yes, I'll obey you in the bedroom, but the rest of my life is my own."

"Agreed," they replied in unison.

"I don't know what you're expecting, but I ought to warn you, I'm not very experienced at sex. I've only ever been with a couple of guys."

"Good." Milo's gaze burned into her profile. "We like inexperience."

"Will I have to have anal sex?" She tried not to shudder at the prospect. "I don't think I'd like that very much."

"Baby, it will blow your mind, but we'll work up to that as well," Hal said. "We'll never make you do anything you're not comfortable with. You have to trust us, and in return it's our responsibility to take care of you."

"Like I said at the start of this conversation," Milo added. "There's no pressure. We'll do our level best to get you out of this terrorist charge, no matter what you decide."

Jodie sat between them, feeling alive and desirable, and a whole raft of other alien emotions. She would do this. There had never really been any serious question of her turning them down, even if she hadn't been completely honest with them. She *had* only been with a couple of guys, that bit was true. What she didn't dare to tell them for fear of them rejecting her was she'd never had an orgasm, other than the self-induced variety. They'd imagine she was frigid if they knew, even though Jodie had read any number of women failed to receive satisfaction through penetrative sex. She just happened to be one of them. It was no big deal. If she could give these two hunks pleasure—one of whose face she always visualized whenever she masturbated—that would be enough for her.

"I'll do it," she said, sharing a decisive gaze between them. "When do we start?"

Both men threw back their heads and roared with laughter. "No time like the present," Milo replied, lifting her straight from her stool and carrying her across the loft. "We need a safety word, darling. Something you'll remember easily. If either of us does anything that makes you uncomfortable, you say that word and it stops."

"Okay."

"What word would you like to use?"

"How about Paddington Green?" she asked with an impish smile.

"That's two words," Hal pointed out. "But I guess it would work."

"What do I call you both?" she asked as Milo kicked a door open, presumably the door to his bedroom.

"Sir or Master works just fine," Hal replied.

"Oh my!"

Milo placed her on her feet and Jodie glanced around the room, truly surprised. It was enormous, and was dominated by the largest bed she had ever seen. It could accommodate four people with ease. She tried not to feel jealous when she thought about the people it had probably accommodated before her, and those that would come afterward. Live for the moment, she reminded herself. The walls were different shades of mauve, light and dark. There was an anteroom off to one side, with the door open. She could see various benches through the opening, but had no idea what use they could be put to. They were unlike the exercise machines she had seen in any gym. There was also an array of implements neatly arranged on shelves along the walls.

"Welcome to our alternative world," Hal said, leaning in for a deep kiss.

When he allowed her up for air, Jodie glanced at Milo, and gasped. He had removed his shirt and sat bare-chested on the edge of the bed, the top button to his jeans undone. She drank in the sight of his muscular torso, and felt a slow smile spread across her face.

"Hey, darlin', don't mind him!"

Hal left her standing where she was, threw off his shirt, and joined Milo on the edge of the bed. Oh lordy, what a view! Hal was as well built as Milo. They made a glorious contrast—Milo dark and brooding, Hal blond and full of good spirits. Both with broad muscular chests, washboard abs. and tapering waists. And they were hers, all hers, for as long as it took.

"What do you require me to do first?" she asked, nervous when they just sat where they were, watching her watching them.

"Excuse me?" Milo frowned at her. "Did someone speak?"

What had she done to displease him? "Oh, I beg your pardon, Master," she replied with a sweet smile. "What would you like me to do for you first?"

"Take off your top. Slowly."

"Yes, Sir."

She pulled it over her head and cast it aside, feeling strangely liberated and not in the least embarrassed. Both men inhaled sharply when she turned to face them again, her breasts encased in their pretty pink prison.

"Now the trousers," Milo said, offering neither compliment nor complaint.

She did as they asked and turned to face them once again, awaiting instructions.

"Keep your eyes lowered," Milo said curtly. "Only look at us when we give you permission to, and speak only when spoken to."

Jodie dropped her gaze to the floor, hoping they wouldn't notice her flimsy panties were soaked clean through with her own juices, and were now worse than useless. A tremor ran through her body as anticipation stoked her desires. Had she really agreed to let both of them fuck her? To have anal sex? To allow them to spank her?

Suddenly, she was full of self-doubt. Perhaps this wasn't such a good idea after all.

"What if I have questions, Sir?" she asked, keeping her eyes lowered. "Can I speak then?"

"We don't want you to have any concerns," Milo replied. "Of course you'll have questions. If they can wait until afterward, that would be best. If not, then say so."

"I will. Sir," she added hastily.

"Shit!" Milo's cell phone rang, breaking the mood. "Talk about bad timing," he said, extracting it from his pocket and checking the display. "It's overseas. Probably for you, darling. Do you want to take it?"

"No, but I suppose I should."

"I'll put it on speaker," Milo said, clearly sensing her reluctance. She nodded, and he did so. "Hanson," he said abruptly.

"Mr. Hanson, my name is Bisset. I believe my daughter's with you."

Chapter Seven

"She is indeed."

The excitement abruptly faded from Jodie's eyes when she heard her father's voice, replaced by an emotion Milo couldn't quite identify. A combination of scorn, susceptibility, and fear, perhaps? Unless Milo missed his guess, Jodie was hell bent on going up against her father simply to get back at him for perceived neglect. She told herself she didn't give a toss about him, and was perfectly prepared to embarrass him. But a part of her feared him, while another part secretly craved his approval.

"I want to thank you for extricating her from this silly misunderstanding. Jodie's still young and can be a little hot headed at times, but she's no terrorist."

Milo recalled meeting Bisset during the infamous oak-tree debacle, but Bisset obviously didn't remember him, and Milo saw no reason to jog his memory. Milo hadn't liked him then and, as he listened to his voice spilling from the tiny phone, talking about damage limitation and headstrong kids, he decided his opinion hadn't changed. Milo let him talk, wondering if he was aware every other sentence contained the words, *Jodie's no terrorist.* He was one of those men who got carried away with his own rhetoric. If you say something often enough then it has to be true. Significantly, he had yet to ask how Jodie was. That fact alone confirmed Jodie's assertion that everything was always about him.

"Jodie's here's now," Milo said when Bisset finally ran out of words. "Would you like to talk to her?"

"Sure."

"Hi, Dad." Jodie crossed her arms defensively over her torso.

"Hey, honey, what have you gotten yourself into this time?"

"I'm fine thanks," she replied with a sarcastic smile Milo wished her father could have seen.

"I've told you before, sugar, these causes of yours are all fine and good, but they only lead to trouble. You'd best get yourself home, and we'll—"

"I can't. The police have my passport."

"Well, I'm sure Mr. Hanson will get things sorted out. Once he has, come back to the States and we'll find you something worthwhile to do."

Milo and Hal exchanged an incredulous glance. Was this guy for real?

"Nothing's changed," Jodie replied curtly. "I'm staying where I am."

A heavy sigh echoed down the line. "Jodie, you really can't carry on like this. If you don't care about yourself, spare a thought for your brother and me."

Milo could see that mention of Paul caused Jodie's confidence to waver. That was a good thing, surely? If she went back to the States, Milo could put his mild infatuation with Jodie behind him, and get on with his life.

Liar!

He felt sorry for her with an old man like that to contend with, but he really didn't want to get involved. Besides, she was committed to her *causes*—causes that definitely didn't jibe with Milo's agenda. He touched his disfigured thigh, reminding himself why, if any reminder were necessary. One glance at her stricken face, and common sense took a hike. He grabbed the phone, took it off speaker, and put it to his ear.

"It's Hanson again, Mr. Bisset. Jodie's in a bit of a state," he said, winking at her. "I don't think she's in the right frame of mind for a parental lecture right now, so I'm going to have to end this call."

"Just a damned minute there, young man. This call ends when I say it does. Now put Jodie back on the line right now."

"Sorry, sir, but that's not going to happen."

"Paul told me you were a good man, but I can see you're just one of those radical types Jodie finds so fascinating. Now put my daughter back on the phone, or I'll find her another lawyer."

"Your daughter's old enough to decide for herself who represents her." Milo glanced at Jodie. Her mouth had dropped open, and she was staring at Milo as though he was the one standing there in his underwear, not her. "Good afternoon to you, sir."

Milo cut the call. "Whoops," he said, patting his knee. "Was it something I said?"

The shadow left Jodie's eye, and she laughed aloud and then scampered over to sit on his knee.

"Sorry about that," he said, kissing the end of her nose. "Now, where were we? Hey, you're trembling. Did he upset you that much?"

"No, it's just he has a way—"

"I know." Milo shared a glance with Hal. "Perhaps this isn't such a good idea tonight. We'll tuck you up in your own bed and we can play when you're feeling less anxious."

"No!" She sat bolt upright, her expression starkly determined. "I'd like to try it right away, before I lose my nerve. Besides, it's the best way I can think of to get my father's voice out of my head."

Hal laughed, reached out a hand, and ran it softly down her thigh. "Can't argue with your logic, babe."

"All right, sweetheart, if you're sure, then the first thing you have to understand is that you're in charge here." Milo's tone was stern. "We give the orders, and we expect you to obey them, but responsibility for your welfare is ours, and we'll never deliberately hurt or humiliate you." He placed the fingers of one hand beneath her chin and tilted her head backward, forcing her to meet his gaze. If she still had doubts, he'd see them in her eyes. She was hopeless at disguising her feelings. All he could see was curiosity and passion swirling in their depths. "Do you understand that?"

"Yes, Sir. I think so."

"That's good, honey. Real good. What you also have to understand is there's a thin dividing line between pain and pleasure. In a sexual context it's a polarity that lives in each of us and the relationship between the two is as profound as it is complex." Milo rubbed her back with soothing sweeps of his hands as he explained. "But we all too often close down our receptors for fear the pain will bring discomfort."

"Right," Hal agreed. "But we're going to teach you that ecstatic and deep pleasure can be ignited by an equal release of intense pain."

Jodie shook her head. "I can't imagine how that could be possible."

She forgot to address him as *sir* but Milo allowed the slip because he didn't want to derail the discussion. It was important she understood what they were going to do, and how to get the most out of it. In fact, seldom had it mattered more for a would-be sub to understand what drove him. Make that never. The restlessness he'd been wrestling with since leaving the service—since the occurrence of the cataclysmic, life-threatening event that had forced him to leave— had abated the moment he kissed Jodie. Given the nature of her *causes* she believed in so passionately, he shouldn't even like her. He definitely shouldn't have felt such an overwhelming need to kiss her. Damn it, what the fuck was she doing to him?

"Sex, pain, and violence all stimulate similar chemicals. Endorphins are released in painful experiences but trick the brain into thinking they're pleasurable." Milo pushed her hair aside and nuzzled her neck. "As you're about to find out. Still wanna play?"

"Yes, Sir, I absolutely do." She looked up at him through a fringe of thick lashes, her eyes glowing with eager fervency.

"Good, just so long as you're sure. Hal, do we have a collar for our sub?"

"I reckon that can be arranged?"

"A collar, Master? May I ask why?"

"You most certainly may, darling. You'll wear it all the time you're in the apartment, as a sign that you belong to Hal and me." He nipped and sucked his way down the long column of her neck, causing her to squirm about on his lap, inflicting considerable damage to his rigid cock. "It will be a visual reminder that you're ours to do with as we please."

Hal returned from the equipment room with a soft leather collar in vibrant red. He fastened it around Jodie's neck and then stood back to examine his handiwork.

"You look pretty as a picture, sweet thing," he said.

Jodie rotated her head, as though getting used to the feel of it, biting her lower lip in a futile attempt to contain a killer smile. Unless Milo read her all wrong, before they even got down to business, she'd already figured out just how much power she actually wielded over the two of them. Milo chuckled. No one could accuse Jodie Bisset of not being a quick study.

"Is it too tight?" Milo asked, deliberately misunderstanding her reaction.

"No, Sir, it feels just fine."

"Wait until we attach a leash to it and have you crawling along at the end of it," Hal said, swooping in for another kiss.

"Good. Now go and stand where you were before the phone interrupted us." Milo tapped her cute butt and she scampered to do his bidding. "Take those panties off, darling. They're soaked through anyway, so they're no use to you."

She hesitated for a beat, then slid them down her legs and stepped out of them.

"Good girl." Both men took a moment to admire her pussy. She didn't wax so they got firsthand confirmation that she was a natural brunette. "Now, what shall we do about that bra? Any suggestions, Hal?"

"I sure have. Pull your tits out of the top of the cups, darling."

Jodie stood with her legs slightly parted as she struggled to comply. She was so going to be a natural at this. The speed with which her embarrassment had disappeared, along with the steady trickle of her own juices slipping down her inner thighs, told him she was both excited and curious. The two men shared an appreciative glance when solid, raspberry-pink nipples poked out above her bra cups. The areolas, too, were raised, crying out to be sucked. Their little sub was more than ready to play.

"Touch your nipples, Jodie," Milo said softly. "Pinch them. Pretend it's one of us doing it for you."

She seemed to forget she wasn't supposed to look at them, and maintained eye contact with them both as she did what they asked. Watching her fingers plucking at her nipples was so damned erotic. Seeing the expression of dark desire that invaded her features caused both men's cocks to solidify painfully, but Milo wasn't ready for Jodie to learn the ugly truth about him. She would be appalled, and very likely put off, so he suffered in silence, and kept his erection zipped inside his pants.

"How does that feel, honey?" Hal asked.

"Strange," she replied in a distant voice. "Sensitive, but nice. I can feel you watching me, and I want to please you."

"That's good, babe." Milo sent her a brief smile. "Okay, that's enough. You can lose the bra now."

She unfastened it without hesitation and threw it aside. Standing naked in front of them, she finally appeared to recall she wasn't supposed to look at them and dropped her gaze, hands crossed almost demurely across her pussy.

"Okay, sweetheart," Milo said. "We're going to spank your butt now, get you used to the feeling. But first Hal's gonna cuff your hands behind you."

Her head shot up. "Why?"

"That would be *why, Sir?* And the reason is so you don't get tempted to touch, at least not with your hands. We like seeing you restrained."

"All right." She paused, glanced up and sent him a mischievous smile that would earn her an extra spanking, the little tease. "Sir."

Hal produced fluffy restraints, walked across to Jodie and kissed her hard and deep. He then told her to put her hands behind her, cuffed her wrists and left her standing there.

"Come over here, Jodie, and bend over my knee," Milo commanded.

She was breathing heavily as she fell across his lap. She was excited, which was good. Milo could work with that. He ran his hand repeatedly across the globes of her ass, stimulating her, talking quietly to her all the time.

"When my hand comes down, it will sting. Roll with the pain, honey, and wait to see what happens. You ready?"

"Yes," she replied breathlessly.

Her hair cascaded over her face as she lay over him. Milo gathered it up and wound it around his fist, tugging gently at the same time as he spanked her with his other hand. He then slipped his spanking hand beneath her and brushed it against her clit. Her body jolted and she let out a startled *oh.*

Milo chuckled. "Oh, indeed."

He repeated the process, spanking her a little harder this time, pulling on her hair just a little more firmly, brushing against her clit for a fraction of a second longer.

"Pleasure and pain," he reminded her. "Can't have one without the other."

"No, Sir," came the breathless reply.

"You've been a real bad girl, and need to be punished."

She moaned when he spanked her for a third time. "Yes, Master, I do."

"How does it feel?"

"You're right. It stings, but then the tingling becomes…well, sensitive, I guess because of where else you're touching me."

"Just think how much greater that rush would be if I spanked you with something stronger than my hand."

"Her pussy's leaking all over your jeans, Milo," Hal said, shaking his head. "She needs to be punished for her lack of control."

"No, she's had enough for the first time."

Milo released her hair, and Jodie mumbled something incomprehensible. He and Hal shared another loaded glance, both of them thinking she was complaining. She wanted her punishment to continue. Shit, she was hot!

He righted her on his lap, curled a hand around her nape above her collar, and forced her head lower, so he could coerce her lips apart with his tongue. Her mouth—there was just something about it. He'd been attracted by it when he first saw her at the police station, which ought to have put him on his guard. It *had*, but he chose to ignore the warning. On a visceral level he guessed he'd always known it would come down to this moment, even when he'd made up his mind that he didn't actually like her, or what she stood for.

Milo sucked her plump lower lip into his mouth, shuddering as he anticipated those same lips wrapped around his throbbing cock. Fuck it, he needed to move this along! Milo prided himself on his staying power, but Jodie was messing with his control, with his mind, with every goddamned part of him. He broke the kiss and told her to kneel in front of Hal. Milo intended to fuck her first, so it seemed only right that Hal got to have his cock sucked. Besides, Milo was keen to watch, and maybe torment her just a little bit while she did her stuff.

Grinning, Hal shed his jeans, sat back down again, and fisted his massive erection.

"Hal could use some help from your mouth," he said curtly. "Get on your knees, babe, and show him how much you care."

She was awkward with her hands cuffed behind her but, to her credit, didn't hesitate to comply. Her hair was in the way when she leaned forward and sipped at Hal's arousal, so Milo got behind her and held it back with one hand. With the other, he played with her ass, repeatedly running a finger down the crack between her cheeks.

"Christ!" Hal sucked in an audible breath. "She's a bit too fucking good at this. I ain't gonna last two minutes."

Milo leaned around her side to get a better look. Her cheeks hollowed out as she filled her mouth with Hal's cock, licking him from its tip right down to his balls, then letting it slide out of her mouth and sucking hard on its head. Fuck not showing himself. Milo couldn't take the pain of being restrained for a moment longer. The lighting in here was dim. If he stayed behind her, she'd never notice his ugly scars. Besides, she was fully occupied servicing Hal.

He briefly released Jodie's hair while he shed his jeans, sighing with relief when his rigid cock finally sprang free from the restricted space. He quickly resumed his position, grabbed her hair again, tugging this time, and ran the tip of his cock down her crack. She made a muffled sound around Hal's erection, and appeared to suck harder. Hal's hips gyrated as he shoved himself deeper into her mouth, and his groans grew in volume. She deserved a reward for working so hard. Milo let her hair go and slid a couple of fingers into her slick cunt. She mewled somehow, even with her mouth so completely full.

"Yeah, you're desperate to have a cock deep inside you, aren't you, sugar?"

"Shit, babe, keep doing that!" Hal's voice was a strangled moan. "I'm gonna cream your throat any second now."

Milo continued to agitate her with his cock against her ass, his fingers working inside her, his thumb rubbing her clit. He felt her spasm at precisely the same time as Hal, and they exploded together. She swallowed down Hal's shower of sperm, her breathing swift and uneven as she rode Milo's fingers and he slapped her ass with his free hand.

When she pulled back and Hal's now half-erect cock slipped from her mouth, Milo helped her to her feet.

"You okay, darling?" he asked.

Jodie sent him a vibrant smile. "Never better," she replied, wiping her mouth with the back of her hand. "This is fun. What happens now?"

Chapter Eight

Jodie hated giving head, absolutely abhorred the taste of a man's sperm, and *never* swallowed. And yet she had so wanted to please Hal, she'd actually enjoyed servicing him. It didn't even occur to her not to swallow. His pleasure communicated itself to her, and she became totally caught up in the moment. Of course, it didn't hurt that Milo was behind her, his hands and cock everywhere as he gave her an orgasm that still had her nerve ends singing several minutes later. Her backside was slightly sore from where Milo had spanked her, but that had been oddly fulfilling, too. Who would have thought that pain could be so rewarding. Perhaps there was something in this pain-pleasure business after all.

Milo sent her a grin that screamed pure, unadulterated sin. It made her gasp. So did seeing him standing sideways on to her, butt naked, an enormous erection jutting aggressively from the juncture of his tapering hips and strong thighs. Both men had an array of scars marring their gorgeous torsos, especially Milo. There was one particularly nasty slash, just below his heart, the marks from the stitches still evident. Battle scars, she supposed, her heart beating erratically as she dwelt upon Milo's close escape.

"What happens next, you ask." He touched his cock and it spasmed beneath his hand. "Hmm, well I figure we need to do something about this baby."

Jodie stood where she was, remembering at the last minute to lower her eyes. She was really getting into the spirit of things now. She knew from his reaction that she had exceeded Hal's expectations. That was rewarding, but she still couldn't quite believe that ten years' worth of dreams were all about to come true, and she would finally get up close and personal with Milo.

"Lie down on the bed," he told her, "on your side."

She did so, and someone released her hands, but not for long. "Raise them above your head, honey," Hal's voice instructed.

She did so and felt them being reshackled. This time the cuffs were fastened to something at the head of the bed. They obviously didn't want her using her hands, but that was okay. She still had her lips, and she'd just learned they were lethal weapons in their own right. The bed dipped behind her and she knew, without looking around, that Milo had joined her. He seemed to get off on always being behind her, like he didn't want her to look at him. Jodie knew she wasn't allowed to make demands, but she wasn't prepared to put up with that situation indefinitely. She *so* wanted to look at, and touch, the man who made the whole world seem like a much better place just by being a part of it.

His large hands ran down the length of her body. Deft fingers reached over her to caress her tits. She groaned when they pinched her nipples, hard enough to bring tears to her eyes.

Tears of joy and expectation.

"You have lovely breasts, darling," he said in a soft caressing voice, his breath peppering her face as he leaned over her body far enough to latch his lips onto one of her nipples.

Jodie closed her eyes, intoxicated by his approval, endeavoring to store every precious second to memory. Who knew what might happen with the ridiculous charges against her? It could only be a matter of time before the police realized she was innocent, especially if her father used his influence, and brought pressure to bear. Milo and Hal could be out of her life again in a matter of days, and that would mean the end of her sensual education. That being the case, Jodie was determined to make the most of every second she spent in their company, and would soak up everything they taught her in the bedroom.

It still astonished her that her strong feelings for Milo allowed space for another man to intrude on their relationship. And yet here she was, and if she had to choose between Milo—whom she had been obsessed with for ten years, or Hal whom she had only just met—she would be hard-pressed to make that choice.

It was totally baffling.

"I figure these babies could use some clamps," Milo said, raising his head from her pebbled nipple and sending her a pussy-clenching grin.

Clamps? She knew what they were, of course, but wouldn't they hurt? Milo's capable hands rubbed something cool into each of her nipples. The feeling was so erotic she forgot all about possible pain, closed her eyes, and lived for the moment.

"Lube," he explained, attaching a clamp carefully to one nipple.

Jodie braced herself for pain that didn't come.

"Oh," she said, blinking back her surprise. "That feels rather nice."

Milo's deep chuckle vibrated through her body. "That's the idea, honey. They restrict the blood flow. Just wait until we remove them again, then you'll get a better idea."

The second clamp was attached and it appeared they were connected by a chain, which Milo tugged on gently. Jodie cried out, opening her eyes wide in surprise as a piquant thrill ripped through her body, stunning her senses.

"Exactly," Milo said, sounding pretty damned pleased with himself. "Now then, Ms. Bisset, I'm gonna lick every inch of you."

"You are?"

"Uh-huh."

And he did. He wouldn't let her move from her side, but proceeded to attack all her most vulnerable places with lips and teeth that knew exactly how to drive her wild. Her heart rate kicked up another notice when he sent a sizzling line of damp kisses down her neck, lapping at the pulse beating at the base of her throat. Her throbbing need blossomed into pure torture, sending delicious shivers up her spine. It was impossible to keep still in the face of such glorious agony, and Jodie expressed her reaction through a series of exaggerated writhes.

"Keep still!" Milo tapped her thigh. Hard. "No one told you to move."

"Sorry, Master."

Jodie immediately stilled, and would remain passive in the face of this all-out assault on her senses if it was the last thing she did. Making Milo pleased with her was the *only* thing that mattered.

Easier said than done, she thought, as his large, hot body remained pressed against her from behind. He worked his way methodically down her torso, his rigid cock still pressing against her back, driving her wild with his skilled tongue and wicked little bites. She trembled and ached, surging on a tide of endless emotion as fire lanced through her veins, wondering if her overstimulated heart could stand so much pleasure without imploding.

"Milo, I can't—"

"Shush, yes you can." He leaned over her, his handsome features looming just above her face, and sent her a smoldering smile that escalated the rate of the delicious desire ripping through her. "Breathe real deep, honey, and let your body absorb it all."

Someone picked up one of her feet and sucked her toes. *Oh my*! It had to be Hal, because Milo's lips were busy working their way along the inside of her lower thigh, exposed when Hal picked up her foot. These guys sure did work well as a team, without the need for words. Of course, her pussy would be opened up for Milo's pleasure now, as well. *Please God, make him get to it soon*! Jodie suppressed a shudder, her body coursing in readiness. She closed her eyes and felt as though she was floating outside of herself—that this was happening to someone else, and she was a casual observer. Make that an interactive observer, she mentally amended, when another spike of lust hit her broadside, causing the muscles in her belly to clench.

She almost elevated from the bed when, without warning, Milo's hand came down hard over her backside. Then, with her leg still elevated, she became aware of his hair tickling her inner thighs as his lips latched onto her clit from behind. She screamed, a combination of pleasure and pain driving her over the edge, and bucked to her second orgasm of the evening, brought on by the pressure of Milo's mouth.

"Responsive little thing, ain't she?" he said, chuckling.

Hal laughed as well, but Jodie figured she wasn't supposed to make any comment. Indeed, speech would have been beyond her, since her body was still trembling with the aftershock—well, all manner of shocks actually—at what Milo had just done to her. At what the pair of them were still doing to her.

Hal had come to lay on one side of her, facing her as he played with the nipple clamps. She heard the sound of a foil packet ripping open and knew the time had come. Finally. She reminded herself that she was good at acting. She wouldn't orgasm with him inside her, but she knew how to pretend. Neither of her previous lovers had guessed she faked it, and neither would these two. Men were funny about stuff like that. It upset their fragile egos if they thought they couldn't satisfy a woman. Jodie wouldn't give them cause to think that way, no matter what.

What would Milo do? Presumably she would be told to roll on her back and he'd cover her. At last she would be able to look at him properly, and reassure herself it really was him.

It didn't happen. Instead, Hal increased the pressure he put on the nipple clamps, while Milo's large body stretched out behind her. His fingers parted her slick folds and, without warning, he slid into her from behind. Hard. Shit, but he was big! He stretched her to capacity, and she desperately wanted to accommodate him, but she was simply too small. Damn, it was *sooo* unfair! All these years she'd waited for this moment, only to fail him miserably.

"Aw, babe, you're so goddamned tight," Milo groaned. "It feels like heaven."

He was right, it did, but that would never be enough for him, would it? He expelled a deep sigh, and then thrust all the way home, his balls slapping against her buttocks almost painfully. Lord above, he'd managed to fit!

"You okay, darling?"

"Yes," she replied breathlessly. "It feels wonderful. I didn't think I'd be able to take you. You're so big, but—"

"Aw, don't tell him that, darling," Hal complained. "We'll never hear the end of it."

"Just don't stop!" Jodie cried, her voice sounding needy, greedy, desperate.

Milo paused, buried deep inside her, and chuckled. "I don't think I could, babe, so if you're planning to use the safe word, you'd better do it quick."

"No, that's the last thing on my mind." *Stop. Why would I want him to stop when finally, after all those dreams, it's actually happening? Milo Hansen is fucking me, and appears to be enjoying himself. So am I, big time.* "Please, Sir."

"Yeah, honey." He stopped moving. "Please what?"

"Hey, you said you wouldn't stop!"

Hal chuckled. "I think the lady's getting impatient."

"Yeah, I got that part."

He started to move again, setting up a punishing rhythm, his hands pulling at her hips to make sure she stayed with him. He needn't have worried. She wasn't going anywhere, and squeezed the muscles of her vagina around him to make sure he knew it. He groaned and picked up the pace some more, the friction intoxicating, inflaming her already overheated blood.

"You feel that, sweet thing? My cock's splitting you in two, and you're just loving it, aren't you?"

"Yes, Sir." She tried to toss her head, but Milo had hold of her hair again. He seemed to enjoy doing that, as though it gave him greater control over her. Did he but know it, he'd controlled her for years. "Please!"

What was she saying? What was she pleading for? She knew, of course. She wasn't quite that naive. She could feel a flickering flame igniting deep within her core, fired by his hot breath against her damp skin, his moans driving her lust.

She was actually going to orgasm!

The sensation intensified, the sound of the fire now raging inside her crashing through her ears, deafening.

"That's it, babe. I can feel it, too. This is so fucking good, but I need you to come for me, darling."

His words caused her whole world to explode like it was the fourth of July. She cried out as brutal passion gripped her, and a glittering starburst erupted deep inside her. She rode his cock with no real sense of rhythm or purpose, desperate to take everything he was offering. Who was the woman crying out to be fucked harder? It sounded like her, but she would never talk that way, would she? The scent of Milo's musky arousal, the feel of his brutal thrusts as his huge cock filled her completely, was enough for her to quit caring. Hal lay directly in front of her, playing with her clamped tits, his eyes shimmering with hot intentions as he watched her climax. My word, was he trying to tell her there was still more to come?

Bring it on!

Milo slowed, waited until her tremors ceased, then picked up the rhythm again. With a series of feral moans, she felt him swell and then stiffen inside her.

"Shit, Jodie!"

He grabbed her hips in a firm grasp, groaning and pulsating as, buried ball-deep inside her, he shot his load into the rubber. His bit her shoulder as he came, his slick body adhering to hers. His excitement was infectious. The muscles in her belly clenched, and she cried out, hardly able to believe it when another orgasm chased the tail of the one that had just ripped through her sensitized body, sending delicious shivers up her spine, and Jodie herself into total meltdown.

She was still laughing, breathless and incredulous when her hands were released, and the nipple clamps were removed. Should she admit that was her first penetrative orgasm—make that orgasms? Yes, definitely she should. They wouldn't laugh. Milo would probably be stoked to know that he'd achieved the impossible. Not that she thought he suffered with self-esteem issues, but still, she wanted to please him.

"Gentlemen," she said, glancing up at them both. "I have an admission to make."

* * * *

Hal ran a strand of Jodie's hair repeatedly through his fingers, drinking in the sight of her flushed face as she looked up at them with a combination of surprise and astonishment in her expression. He had a feeling he knew what she was about to say. He glanced at Milo, flat on his back, bathed in sweat, and looking pretty damned pleased with himself. He'd probably guessed, too.

"What's that then, babe?" Hal asked, feigning ignorance.

"Well, you have to promise not to laugh, but that's the first orgasm I've ever had through penetrative sex."

Milo, still flat out, blew her a kiss. "All that says is you've chosen pretty selfish men in the past."

"No, you don't understand. I thought I couldn't…you know. A lot of women can't, and still live perfectly fulfilled lives."

Hal laughed. "That's 'cause they don't know what they're missing. What you've never had you can't get upset about, or some such shit."

"Perhaps it was a fluke." Jodie eyes sparkled as she glanced at Hal's half-erect cock, and then bit her plump lower lip.

"That's just the sort of talk that'll earn you another spanking," Milo warned, sitting up and dealing with the condom. "I'll go get the shower running."

Now something *had* surprised Hal. He leaned up on one elbow, and sent Milo a probing look. "You sure?" he asked softly.

"Yeah." His back was to Hal, and he shrugged, a little too casually. "It's no big deal."

But it was to Milo, and Hal knew it. He watched his best mate walk naked toward the bathroom, then looked down at Jodie, and shook his head. Milo had done what he always did—which was either fuck from behind, blindfold his sub, or both. He was sensitive about his scars, didn't like answering questions about them, hated being pitied, and *never* let women see him in the shower. There was obviously something about Jodie that had broken through his barriers. Hal hadn't fucked her himself yet, but he could still relate to that.

"Come on, babe." Hal stood and reached out a hand to help Jodie up. "Let's get you cleaned up."

The shower stall in Milo's bathroom was easily big enough for the three of them. By the time Jodie and Hal joined him, Milo already had the room full of steam. Hal wondered if that was deliberate. It was difficult to know what Milo was thinking at that particular moment because this was uncharted territory.

The moment Jodie stepped into the stall Milo pulled her into his arms, kissing her hard and deep. Then put her aside so he could squirt bodywash onto his hands. He lathered it up and applied the fragrant foam to her back. Hal washed his own body, waiting to see what happened.

Milo paused, clearly feeling the need to do more kissing than scrubbing. They pair of them stood with water cascading over their heads, their bodies and lips fused together. When Milo finally released Jodie it happened, and Milo must have known that it would. She dropped her eyes and even through the thick steam she was close enough to see Milo's deep, ugly scar, the skin rough and discolored, that ran from his right hip halfway down his thigh.

"Milo!" She clapped a hand over her mouth. "Whatever happened?"

"Fortunes of war," he replied, not looking at her.

Milo was probably waiting for her to show repulsion. No matter what Hal tried to tell his buddy on the subject, he was convinced it would put women off. Hal figured that if it did, they weren't women worth knowing. If he brought women home, he never put himself in a position where they would see, not only the scars but, in spite of his tireless efforts to build it up again, the fact that his right thigh had a dent in it and was slightly smaller than his left.

The torrent of questions Hal had expected didn't materialize. Instead, Jodie stood on her toes, placed a gentle kiss on Milo's lips, like it was no big deal, then turned and did the same thing to Hal. *Atagirl*! It was exactly the right way to react, and Hal wanted to applaud. Had Milo sensed, on some visceral level, that Jodie would respond that way? There was something special about her that set her apart from the many women he and Milo had shared over the years. Still, no point getting carried away. Even if he and Milo decided to settle down, Jodie couldn't be the one because she'd made it patently clear that she had no intention of giving up her causes.

Milo shut off the water, stepped out of the shower first, and wrapped a towel around his waist, covering what he considered to be a deformity. He held out another towel and wrapped Jodie in it when she emerged. He wound a second one around her head, turban style, and then vigorously set about drying her entire body. Hal dried himself off, watching them both closely. He could sense that Jodie was bursting with curiosity, but had the good sense to keep her mouth shut.

"Let's get back to bed," Milo said, smiling at Jodie. "You look beat."

"Oh, I'm not *that* tired."

Milo slapped her butt, but the blow was protected by the thick towel covering her torso. "You've had enough for your first lesson."

"Don't I have any say in that?"

"Seems our little playmate has forgotten the first rule already," Milo said, addressing the comment to Hal over Jodie's head.

"Yep, looks that way." Hal flexed a brow. "Course, she might just be angling after another spanking."

"Uh-huh." Milo shook a finger beneath Jodie's nose. "Ain't gonna happen, babe. We have to take this slow."

Only now that he was relaxed, and typically in control again, did Hal realize how tense Milo had actually been in the shower. Jodie's *no big deal* reaction to his leg had scored her points with Milo, and it seemed they were about to break another taboo. They often shared a woman in Milo's room, since it was larger than Hal's and equipped with everything they needed, but they never showered or slept the night with her. Milo had never said why that was, but Hal figured he didn't want a woman seeing his "deformity" in the cold light of day.

"Here you go, honey," Milo said. "Sit yourself down and I'll brush your hair out for you."

He did so, while Hal sat on the bed and watched. First Milo toweled her long hair vigorously, then he pulled a brush through it until it was tangle-free.

"You okay sleeping with damp hair, or do you need me to dry it for you?" Milo asked.

"No, I'm good like this." She hid a wide yawn behind her hand, and then grinned at them both. "Seems I am pretty beat after all. Can't imagine why."

Hal pulled back the covers and ushered Jodie into the center of the bed, relieving her of the towel that covered her torso as he did so. Milo climbed in on her opposite side—the side that ensured his left thigh was up against her. Hal took the other side.

"Hey, thanks for tonight," Milo said, leaning up on one elbow to kiss her gently. "You were, as they say on your side of the pond, awesome."

"That goes for me, too," Hal agreed, kissing her as well. "Sleep well, honey."

Chapter Nine

Jodie woke abruptly from a deep sleep, feeling rested and up for whatever the day threw at her. But not quite yet—she was way too comfortable to move a muscle. She wriggled down, closed her eyes, and allowed herself the luxury of waking up again slowly. She thought about what she'd so recklessly done the night before with Milo and Hal, and waited for the guilt to kick in.

It didn't happen.

Seeing Milo's injuries had been a shock, to put it mildly. Something really bad had happened to him, obviously, disfiguring his gorgeous body. She sensed his reluctance to allow people to see the ugly results. That, presumably, was why he had remained behind her while he'd fucked her. She had so wanted to ask him about it, but sensed it would have been a mistake, so she treated him like it was no big deal.

And her reward had been to spend the night, sandwiched between two hot, muscular bodies, feeling safer, more protected, more cared for than at any other time in her life. Milo's chest acted as her pillow for half the night. Hal threw an arm possessively across her torso, which felt fine and right to Jodie. This morning she felt satiated, pleasantly sore, and eager for her next lesson. She suppressed a giggle, wondering if the drug companies were aware that sharing two virile men was the best sleeping pill on the market. Maybe she should patent the idea. The thought made her smile. It would really give her dad something to get mad at her about.

She had no idea how long she had slept, but when she turned on her side Milo's part of the bed was empty and cold. She panicked for a moment, then sensed the weight of Hal's body on her opposite side, and relaxed again. She opened her eyes and his face loomed above hers. Blond hair flopped across his brow as he leaned up on one elbow, a speculative smile flirting with his lips as he watched her wake up.

"Hey, morning, sleepyhead," he said, leaning in for a kiss.

Jodie stretched, wiggled her toes, and grinned up at Hal. So it really had happened. She hadn't dreamed it all. "What time is it?"

"Gone nine."

"Heavens, I did sleep for a long time. Where's Milo?"

"He went for a jog, came back and showered, now he's got to be in court. He has a client coming up before the magistrates this morning."

"He did all that, and I didn't hear a thing?" She widened her eyes. "How come?"

Hal chuckled. "He moves like a panther when it suits him. I guess he thought you'd earned your rest, and didn't want to disturb you. I'm under orders to make sure you report to the police station this morning."

Jodie winced. "Thanks for the reminder."

"Hey, we've got time yet."

Hal pushed the covers back, exposing her nakedness. Jodie resisted the urge to cover herself with her hands. Instead she met his gaze and sent him a question with her eyes. When did she get to be so brazen? His own eyes darkened to a deep midnight blue in response, and he let out a soft whistle.

"Has anyone ever told you that you've got one hell of a body?"

She sent him a glittering smile, her self-consciousness falling away in light of his obvious approval. "Can't say they have. I don't reveal it to just anyone, you know."

"Yeah, I do know." He ran a finger lazily down the side of her breast, causing the nipple to harden without him even having to touch it. "Come here, darling, and let me wake you up properly."

Hal sat up and pulled her into his arms so abruptly the breath left her lungs in an extravagant whoosh. His tongue, velvety and sensuous, teased the corners of her mouth and then worked its way inside, assured and demanding. The kiss quickly grew heated, as did Jodie's body. Hal's hands swept down her sides, coming to rest on the edges of her breasts—breasts that were squashed against his chest, soft and pliant against the solidity of his muscular torso. Hal groaned around their fused lips, deepening the kiss as he pulled her bodily across his legs. He was very erect. She could feel his cock pulsating against her pussy, filling her with a paradox of pleasure and longing, causing her to wonder how long it would be before it filled all of her.

He reached up and took full possession of her breasts, tugging at nipples that were still slightly sore from the night before. Not that she cared. She arched her back, increasing the friction, making Hal smile at her obvious need.

"You were born for stuff like this," he said, his voice soft, his eyes full of admiration as he leaned forward and took a nipple into his mouth, biting gently.

Jodie rested her hands on his chest and pushed down on her arms until they were fully extended. A vortex of desire, tingling exhilaration, and old-fashioned lust spangled though her, sending her body into sensory overload. She must look a total mess, having gone to bed with wet hair that probably now stuck up all over the place like an angry witch's. Who gave a shit? She closed her eyes as Hal's skilled mouth, his addictive scent, and the sexual magnetism that radiated from him caused a deep ache to blossom between her legs.

Just when she thought she couldn't take anymore, he released her nipple and tipped her off of him.

"Get on your hands and knees," he ordered curtly.

Jodie wondered if he planned to fuck her ass, surprised at how much a prospect that would once have appalled her now caused her juices to flow. She heard a drawer open, and then the ripping of a foil packet. Hal positioned himself behind her, and slapped her butt hard.

He repeated the process half a dozen times, each blow a little harder. He didn't compensate by touching her clit in the way that Milo had the day before, but it didn't seem to matter. She cried out each time a fresh slap rang out, but not because it hurt. She barely felt the pain because it was overwhelmed by the anticipation that roiled through her like an angry volcano about to blow.

"Your arse sure does look pretty, now it's all pink," he said, reaching beneath her and gouging at her dangling tits. "Open your legs, darling."

As soon as she did so, panting with expectancy, Hal parted her folds and entered her with one assured thrust. They both groaned as he filled her to capacity, and set up a steady rhythm.

"Hold your position, darling," he said breathlessly, "and let's really fuck. You like it hard, don't you?"

"Yes," she replied breathlessly, thinking it was true. How come she hadn't known that about herself before now? "The harder the better."

The physical alchemy that had existed between her and Milo the night before seemed to flow just as strongly with her and Hal. That didn't surprise Jodie. If she could feel for Hal the way she always had for Milo, there had to be a reason for it, but now wasn't the time to get all philosophical.

The hot brand of Hal's swollen cock rammed deep inside her, stretching her to the limit, flamed her blood. She cried out, and pushed back against him, greedy to take as much of him as he could give her. Perspiration bathed her body, and a low, animalistic sound slipped past her lips. He was splitting her in two, but it still wasn't enough for her. It would never be enough. What the hell was happening to her?

"That's it, honey. Now you have it all."

"You're filling me, Hal. I can't believe how well you fit."

Hal laughed. "Get used to it, honey."

Get used to it?

Hal drove himself harder and faster, leaving Jodie wondering if she would orgasm again, as she had with Milo the night before, or whether that had actually been the one-off she hoped it wasn't. She wasn't left in ignorance for long. She felt the now familiar kernel of primitive sensation uncurling deep in her core, and pushed back to meet Hal's next thrust, keen to make it flower. Hal chuckled and slapped her ass in between thrusts.

"Greedy!"

"Sorry, Master," she replied, panting. "I can't help it."

"It's okay, darling. I'm close, too. Let's do this together."

Hal withdrew almost all the way, his cock agitating the sensitive walls of her pussy, driving her wild. Then he thrust in again, hard and deep, his breathing labored as he worked her cunt like a man on a mission, reaching beneath her as he did so to play with her thrumming clit. It worked like a charm, and Jodie felt herself starting to fragment.

"Hal, I can't hold it!"

"It's okay, babe. Come for me."

He gave one more deep thrust, and it was her undoing. She closed her eyes and screamed his name, abandoned, gripped by her inexorable need as pleasure exploded through her body. The tremors had barely ceased before Hal slapped her butt again, groaned, and shot his load.

"Geez, babe," he said, cradling her in his arms afterward, waiting for his breathing to return to normal. "That was something else."

Jodie blinked up at him. "I think that's supposed to be my line."

They took a moment to recover, then showered.

"Take your time dressing," Hal said, kissing her. "I'll have breakfast made by the time you're ready. I'm betting you're hungry."

She smiled at him, feeling flighty and flirtatious. "Whatever makes you say that?"

* * * *

Hal hummed to himself as he clattered about in the kitchen, wondering what Jodie would prefer to eat. She'd devoured Milo's fry-up the previous day, but didn't strike Hal as the sort of girl who made a habit out of heavy cooked breakfasts. He settled for fluffy scrambled eggs on toast, along with juice, fresh fruit, and yogurt.

He thought about what they'd just done as he worked, still reeling from the profound effect it had had on him—way more so than with any other woman he could remember. In fact she touched him profoundly on all levels, in bed and out of it. She could have been *the* one, but for the fact...

Jodie burst into the room, intruding upon his thoughts, looking fresh as summer in jeans and a sleeveless top, her feet bare, their red collar still around her neck. Her hair was damp and fell halfway down her back in a riot of disorderly curls. Her freckles stood out across her nose, looking so damned adorable in a face that shone with the afterglow of mind-blowing sex. Her lips looked swollen from his kisses, her eyes held an awareness that hadn't been there the previous day, and there was a subtle alteration in her entire persona. This was a lady who liked what she'd just discovered about her passionate nature.

"Hey, babe." Hal poured coffee for them both. "You okay? We weren't too rough with you?"

She sent him a radiant smile and slipped onto a barstool. "You were just perfect. So is this meal."

"Help yourself."

They sat and ate in companionable silence for a while.

"You have questions, I expect," Hal said when she pushed her plate aside.

"I'm still reeling from what happened to me, to be honest. You guys really lit my fire."

"Glad to be of service, ma'am."

"I still feel a little bit...well, naughty, I suppose, to have taken you both on."

"Never feel guilty or ashamed about what you do, honey. What happens between consenting adults behind closed doors is no one else's business." He sent her his sexiest smile. "Rule of thumb, if it feels right, go for it."

She returned his smile with an enticing grin of her own. It went straight to Hal's cock, which stood up, ready for more action. "I don't think I exactly showed any restraint."

The corners of Hal's mouth lifted. "No, we figured you probably wouldn't." He patted her knee. "We're not usually wrong about these things."

She blew air through her lips, trying and failing to look affronted. "What can I possibly say to that?"

"It was just an observation," Hal replied, amused by her reaction.

"I need to let you into a little secret." She bit her lower lip. "Well, a big one, actually."

"Okay, I'm all ears."

"Well, this will sound whacky, but I've been carrying a torch for Milo for ten years now, ever since he caught me when I fell out of that tree."

She sent him a *there, I've said it* look, defying him to laugh. Hal didn't. "Why Milo?" he asked instead. "I gather there were quite a few guys there at the time, including Raoul."

"Milo was the one who actually caught me. The others laughed, but he was so concerned about me. He carried me into the house, reassured me, told me my wrist was only sprained, put ice on it." She shrugged self-consciously. "I was twelve, and thought he was *the* most sophisticated man I'd ever met. We'd just moved back to the States from somewhere or other, and Dad promised we wouldn't be leaving again. Two weeks later he got posted to the embassy here in London. I knew Milo was British and, to my twelve-year-old brain, it was a sign." This time she laughed. "Obviously, he'd wait for me to grow up, then we'd ride off together into the sunset."

"Is that why you insisted upon remaining in England to finish your education?"

"No, not really...well, perhaps partly." She sent him an impish smile from beneath her fringe of thick lashes. "I just liked England, the English education system, everything about the country. I suppose I was fed up with being a gypsy and felt the need to put down roots, have permanent friends somewhere. Dad promised this time we really were going back to the States for good, but I'd heard it all before and didn't believe it." She shrugged. "Turns out he was telling the truth for once."

Hal stretched. "Must have come as quite a shock when Milo turned up at the police station to bail you out."

"And then some." She shook her head. "I didn't think he remembered who I was, but it seems he did."

"Honey, I doubt you'd be too easy to forget, even at age twelve."

"Well, he might remember me, but he doesn't like me much. Why is that?"

Hal raised both brows. "After what happened between the three of us last night, you think he doesn't like you?"

"I feel like...oh, I don't know, like he did that almost in spite of himself."

"Don't put yourself down, sweetheart. It must be obvious that Milo and I often play together in that room, *but* he never shares the shower with any of the women we take there, and he never sleeps the night with them, either."

"Oh."

"Oh, about covers it. You've obviously gotten to him."

"His scars, I suppose." She leaned her chin in her cupped hand. "What happened to him?"

Hal wasn't sure whether to tell her. It wasn't his story to tell. Milo never would, but must have known that having seen his leg she would have questions. If he hadn't wanted Hal to answer them, he would have made that clear.

"If you got the impression he doesn't like you, you're wrong. It's your causes he has issues with."

"But why?" Jodie wrinkled her brow. "I'm only trying to make a difference."

"Your intentions are good but, at the risk of sounding patronizing, you don't really have any idea what it's like in these places. Don't get on your high horse," he said, flapping a hand at her, sensing her angst. "Long story short, a unit of the SAS, including Milo and me, were in Afghanistan three years ago. Why we were there isn't important. I couldn't tell you anyway. What I can tell you is we were in a remote village that had been sacked, leaving the sort of people you care about—women who'd been raped, and young kids—homeless and starving." Hal paused, lost in a version of hell he'd spent the last three years trying to forget. "We were battle hardened, immune to most of the shit we came across, but even we were moved by what we saw this time. So, we decided to forget our orders and try to move the worst of the refuges to a place of safety."

Her eyes widened. "That's a real good thing to do."

"It would have been, except one of the women, wrapped head to toe in a burka, started screaming blue murder and lobbed a live grenade at us."

"Oh, shit! Is that what happened to Milo?"

"Yep." Hal swallowed. "I thought I'd lost him. That damned grenade just missed his femoral artery. If it had hit, it would have been good night, Vienna. No way could we have got him to a field hospital in time. As it was, the blast robbed him of a good chunk of his thigh. He was in therapy for months and, I gotta tell you, at one stage we thought he wouldn't walk probably again. Course, the doctors didn't take into account just how fucking stubborn he is." Hal noticed tears in Jodie's eyes. "He pushed himself to the limit and beyond, endured endless skin grafts and loads of other stuff, and now you'll only see a very slight limp when he's tired."

"That's so sad." She shook her head and wiped away the tears. "I wonder why he let me see."

Hal wondered the same thing.

"I expect the woman was confused. She probably thought you guys were going to hurt her as well."

Hal's expression hardened. Jodie had just demonstrated why there was no future for them with such a liberal-minded non-realist. "She knew exactly who we were, and what we were trying to do for them. She died in the blast herself, so did some of the other women and kids."

"Oh no!"

"Save your pity for where it belongs," Hal said curtly. "Some people just don't want to be helped."

She looked up at him, and shook her head. "I'm sorry. That came out all wrong. It must have been a nightmare for you guys."

Hal wasn't ready to be appeased. "You could say that."

"Is that why you both left the service?"

"Milo wasn't physically fit enough to remain in the SAS. We were all on a charge for disobeying orders and risking the mission, and...well, we were thoroughly disillusioned by then, anyway. It seemed like it was the right time to pack it in."

"With good reason. No wonder he was so opposed to my efforts, but I still think they can work if enough people get behind them. Just because one evil woman tried to take Milo out...I mean, we don't know why she did that."

"Precisely, we don't know, because we don't live in their part of the world." Hal felt anger radiate through his body. She just didn't get it. "And don't properly understand their beliefs and what they're prepared to sacrifice in their name. It's rather arrogant to assume that the whole world wishes to live by the same standards as the West."

"Yeah, I guess." Jodie looked crestfallen. "But I can't abandon what I think is right. Not for anyone." She sighed, and added softly, "Not even for Milo."

"I guess that's up to you."

"How did you guys get to be so tight?" she asked after a brief pause. "I don't mean to be rude, but you look and sound as though you're from different walks of life."

"Milo's upper class and I'm just a working boy from the backstreets?" he suggested, a hint of a smile breaking through his anger.

"Well, that is how it seems to an outsider, and yet it's as though you can communicate without the need for words. I'm guessing, but I don't think you discussed taking me to bed. You just seemed to exchange a look, and knew you were on the same page."

"Yeah, that's pretty much how it is with us. Milo's family owns half the county of Kent…well, I exaggerate, but they certainly have a huge old house down there that will be Milo's one day. He's an only child, you see. He went to Harrow, then on to Oxford, where he got his law degree. Then he signed up for the army, determined to prove something to himself by getting into the SAS. He could have gone in as an officer, and had a relatively easy time of it, but he chose to do it the hard way."

"That doesn't surprise me."

"He and I were on the same basic training course, and hated each other. I thought he was too soft to make the grade, he thought I was a total jerk. Neither of us was right." Hal laughed. "We just kinda hit it off when we were paired together on a night exercise. He actually saved me from major embarrassment when I wandered into quicksand."

"And what do you do now he's practicing law?"

"I act as his investigator. Basically we live, work, and play together, and that's the way we like it."

"It must be nice to have such a close friend."

The pathos in her tone caused Hal's annoyance with her ideology to dissipate. "Yeah well, we'd best get you down to the police station," he said, stacking their dirty plates in the dishwasher. "You…er, might wanna remove that collar."

Jodie reached up a hand and touched it. "Not a chance. It's mine."

Hal laughed. "As you wish."

There was tension between them as Hal drove to the station. Partly, he assumed, because Jodie was anxious about reporting in, but partly caused by Hal's withdrawal from her. He was being unfair, he knew that, but he felt torn. Never had he met a woman who so comprehensively drew him in, but he and Milo had always said in the unlikely event of them settling down, they would share the same woman—just like they shared every other aspect of their lives. Jodie could very likely be that woman, except for her fucked-up view of the world's problems. Milo would never go for it, and Hal didn't want to put him in the position of having to seriously consider it.

And if he knew how smitten Hal was, Milo *would* consider it. Their friendship, their shared history, made that inevitable.

"We're here," he said, sliding the car into a multistory a few streets away. "Wear your dark glasses, honey, and keep your head down."

"You think there will be reporters?"

"There usually are, and news of your arrest will have got out by now. Daddy won't be best pleased if your picture's plastered all over the dailies. Milo's arranged for us to go in around the back, but still."

"And we don't want to disappoint, Daddy, do we?" She clenched her jaw. "Okay, I'm ready."

"That isn't precisely what I meant."

"Then what?"

"You've made yourself conspicuous by getting arrested."

"Which wasn't my intention." Jodie's tone was scathing. "I'm not the one in my family seeking public recognition."

"Think about it." Hal placed a guiding hand on her elbow as they covered the short distance to the police station. "You were doing what you wanted to do, without anyone being any the wiser. But now—"

"Oh shit, I get what you mean." Jodie's face paled. "Now everyone will know who I am, or more to the point, who my father is." She shook her head. "Great, just great!"

"And that will make you a target," Hal said, determined to tell her the brutal truth. "You'll put yourself and others in danger if you sail too close to the wind over sensitive issues."

"Shit," she muttered again as they made their way inside.

Their business didn't take long. Hal ushered Jodie out through the back entrance again, pleased to have avoided the press. He pushed the door open, sensing that Jodie had relaxed as well, and was met with a plethora of camera flashes.

"Goddamn it! Keep your head down." He grabbed Jodie's arm and hustled her away. "How the fuck did they get back here?"

Chapter Ten

Milo's case at the magistrate's court dragged on, and he found it hard to concentrate. Eventually it was done. He shook his client's hand, aware the guy was lucky to get off with a slap on the wrist and a modest fine. He checked his cell phone for messages, and found one from Hal, telling him to call, urgently.

"What's up?" he asked when Hal picked up.

"Reporters lying in wait outside the nick," Hal replied tersely.

"Shit, how the fuck…"

"My thoughts exactly."

"Presumably they knew it was Jodie."

"Oh yeah. There were only two of them, but they called her name and she looked up before I could stop her."

"Damn. You back home yet?"

"On our way now."

"Okay, I'll be with you in ten. We'll talk about it then."

The downside of living in Battersea was the lack of a nearby underground station. Milo took a cab home. It was quicker and cheaper than trying to drive and then find a parking space. He mulled over Jodie's situation as he sat in the cab, stuck in traffic on the Albert Bridge. Thoughts of the hot sex they'd enjoyed the night before had been messing with his brain all the morning, and showed no signs of abating. She was a confusing combination of ideology, vulnerability, anger, and sexy, desirable female. Milo should have done what he could for her from a legal perspective and walked away. The moment he offered to let her stay with him and Hal—and he still didn't know what had made him do that—walking away was never going to be an option.

Why her, with her admirable but totally misguided ambitions? Not that she'd ever see them in that light, so he should have left her the fuck alone. It was too late for that now. Damn, just the thought of her pussy clenching around his cock, the cute mewling noises she made when she was close, her curiosity about the games he and Hal wanted to play with her, her intoxicating sensuality, told him stuff about her passionate nature she probably hadn't been aware of herself.

He had felt a deep, bewildering oneness with her the first time he'd seen her in that grimy police station, and now he was in deep. He wanted her with an intensity that shook him rigid. After all, he'd only known her for a day. Lightning didn't strike that quickly, did it? He cared about her, too, in a way that he never had for any other woman. He also felt sympathy for the situation she found herself in with her dysfunctional family, and could understand why she wanted to rebel against them.

But they were poles apart in every other aspect of their lives, apart from sex, of course. They were pretty damned compatible in that regard, but the principles that had formed his character and made Milo the man he was today were diametrically opposed to Jodie's take on life. She wasn't just playing at championing the world's underprivileged—she was deadly serious about it—and Milo absolutely couldn't go back there.

His leg spasmed, as it still did occasionally—a sure sign he'd overdone it. It was also a timely reminder of just why anything other than a passing fling with Jodie was out of the question. His physical scars had healed—after a fashion—but the mental damage done by that fucking grenade still gave him nightmares. In the beginning he had woken up regularly, screaming, drenched in sweat, the sheet twisted around him like a straitjacket, his subconscious dragging him back to the time and place he most wanted to forget. Those incidents were gradually getting less frequent now but he absolutely didn't need the constant reminders that Jodie's "well-intentioned by basically naively impractical" campaigns would engender.

That he was even considering anything other than one of their usual flings brought him up short. How had that happened? Presumably that's why he'd showered with her. It was a test he hadn't consciously decided upon, but she'd passed it with flying colors, expressing nothing more than mild concern about his scars, wisely asking no intrusive questions. Presumably she had saved those for Hal this morning. Milo wondered if he'd answered them, rather hoping that he had. If Jodie knew the truth then she would realize for herself that this was nothing heavy, always supposing her thoughts had even veered in that direction.

The cab pulled up outside the apartment block. Milo paid the driver, noticing Hal's car was back in its usual spot. He let himself in and rode the elevator up to the loft. Hal and Jodie were seated at the breakfast bar, sharing a pot of coffee.

"Hey." He dropped his document case on the couch, but resisted the urge to touch Jodie. "I hear you've been on candid camera this morning," he said to her.

"I had no idea I was so popular," she replied with a casual shrug.

She looked up at him, huge eyes brimming with an emotion he didn't try to put a name to, and felt his groin constrict. Damn it, perhaps her causes were just a passing phase. They could work something out, surely? Seeing her here in his and Hal's private space—a space where they seldom invited anyone to stay for more than one night—felt so fundamentally right.

"Did you find out which papers the photographers were from?" Milo asked Hal, helping himself to coffee.

"No, I didn't recognize them, and didn't want to stop and ask. That would have given them more opportunities to snap away at Jodie."

"Good point." Milo leaned against the kitchen surface, ankles crossed, and rubbed his jaw as he thought it through. "We know most of the regular snappers, so I'm guessing they were freelance, working on a tip-off."

"From inside the nick?"

"Most likely."

"The police would tell the press?" Jodie's eyes were luminous with shock, outrage, anger.

Milo shook his head. She really was hopelessly naïve. "In a heartbeat, darling. Half of England's finest earn a bit extra by letting the press know if anything interesting goes down in the station."

She shrugged. "Oh."

"Ah well." Milo loosened his tie and shrugged out of his suit jacket. "I guess we'll never know."

Hal took his phone from his pocket and scrolled through the pictures on it. "Seemed only right to return the favor," he said, grinning as he handed the phone to Milo. "I snapped them snapping us."

Milo laughed. Leave it to Hal to turn the tables. He looked at the pictures, then shook his head. He didn't recognize the guys, either. "Send it to my e-mail."

"Will do. You got ideas?"

"Not sure." Milo turned to Jodie. "I guess your dad won't be best pleased if your picture's all over the press, and the web, so I have to at least attempt damage limitation."

Jodie shrugged, like she didn't much care, but the gesture looked contrived. She was trying just a little bit too hard not to appear concerned, which told him deep down her father's reaction mattered to her, even if she wasn't ready to admit it to herself.

Milo spent half his working life talking to people accused of committing crimes, and could almost always tell if they were being completely honest. In Jodie's case, she was holding something back. Still, if it had nothing to do with the circumstances leading up to her arrest then he figured it was none of his damned business. He definitely didn't want to get into the minefield that was her relationship with her family. That would imply an intention to prolong their relationship, which wasn't going to—which couldn't—happen.

He caught sight of her lovely profile and his heart stalled. She looked up, saw him gawping at her, and her face colored. Then she sent him a wicked little smile that fired his blood. Shit, she'd really gotten beneath his skin! Part of him wanted it to take a while to finalize her affairs, just so she would have to stay with them a little bit longer. The practical side of his brain told him to get over himself.

"Excuse me for a moment."

Milo broke eye contact with her before he could start daydreaming about that temptingly plump lower lip of hers, and all the things he'd like to have her do with it—to him. He went into his bedroom, trying not to look at the bed and think about what had gone down there the night before. *Yeah, right!* He quickly changed into jeans and a T-shirt, thrust his bare feet into Docksiders, and splashed water on his overheated face.

Back in the main room, he decided the only way to get through this with his sanity intact was to keep it all business.

"Okay, guys," he said. "We'll knock together some lunch. Then I need you to go over to the house in Camden Town, Hal."

"Thought you might."

"Talk to the owners, Phil and Betty?" Milo glanced at Jodie to make sure he'd got their names right, and she nodded. "See if they have any ideas how those papers relating to Spectrum got to be in their house. I don't hold out much hope, but we have to try."

"Right, I'm on it." Hal winked at Jodie. "But first, tuna mayo okay for you all?"

"Great," Jodie replied. "Can I help?"

"Nah, you're good. I can just about manage to make a sandwich."

"I could get used to being spoiled," Jodie said with a self-conscious little laugh. "I'll just grab my laptop then and catch up on my e-mail."

"Don't respond to anything to do with your causes," Milo said when she returned.

She stopped walking, and glared at him. "You're kidding me?"

"Darling, the police will be tracking your account, or least we have to assume they will be. Your cell phone, too, for that matter. Don't forget, if you communicate with anyone connected with your arrest, however innocently, it'll give the police the excuse they're looking for to re-arrest you."

"Okay, okay, I get it." Jodie put down her computer and threw up both hands, looking annoyed. "I'll just put my life on hold and wait for this to blow over."

God, she's young! "No going into any websites to do with your causes, either." Milo fixed her with a firm glare. "Those will be monitored, too."

"That's *so* unfair. There's stuff I need to keep up with."

"Welcome to the real world," Milo replied with a cynical twist to his lips.

"I've made commitments, and I'm waiting for final news about something. People are depending upon me."

"About what?" Milo asked, scowling. She really was into all this stuff in a big way.

"Well, I guess it'll keep."

Milo was being distant and professional. He could see that she was confused, and perhaps a little hurt by his attitude. He didn't want it to be that way. He would much prefer to throw her onto the nearest surface and fuck her senseless.

It wasn't going to happen now, but with her under his roof indefinitely, Milo had absolutely no idea how long he would be able to keep his distance. Take it one day—one hour—at a time, he told himself, just like when he'd been in the service. That mantra had worked for him then, but he wouldn't take bets on it doing the same thing now. Jodie had got him in a major tailspin and he no longer knew which way was up. Fuck it, he should have booked her into a hotel and been done with it. Whatever had he been thinking?

"Lunch," Hal called from the kitchen, sending Milo a probing glance, probably because he was acting so out of character.

They ate mostly in silence, the lunchtime news playing on the television behind them with the sound muted. Milo wanted to see if there was anything on it about Jodie. There wasn't, at least not yet.

"Okay," Hal said, gathering up his phone and keys. "I'm outta here. Play nice without me, children."

Without Hal's cheerful chatter to break the tension, it seemed unnaturally quiet in the loft. Milo was aware of Jodie's hurt expression as she pottered about tidying the kitchen, avoiding making eye contact with him. Milo owed her an explanation for the barriers he'd put up, but didn't attempt one. How could he explain when he didn't understand himself?

"I have work to do," he said, heading for his study. "Shouldn't take more than a couple of hours. It's a nice afternoon. Why don't you sit out on the terrace, catch a few rays? There're books and stuff over there if you need something to read."

"I'm fine." She inverted her chin and headed for the terrace. "You don't have to entertain me."

Oh baby, if you knew how much I want to! Milo fired up his laptop, and went through the procedures to make sure it was clean. Then he sent an e-mail to Raoul, attaching the picture of the photographers who had snapped Jodie, wondering if Raoul had anything on them in his extensive records. There was something not quite right about the guy on the left. He and Hal knew all the press photographers, including the freelancers. Jodie's story was a big deal, so it wouldn't be newbies who just happened to snap her leaving the nick. It would be someone with decent contacts, or with an axe to grind.

If it was the latter, then Raoul would almost certainly know. Raoul's files would be the envy of the security services on both sides of the pond, had they known about them. Hopefully they would come through for them this time, just as they had so often in the past.

* * * *

Jodie felt tired and dispirited. She wanted to ask if she'd done something to sour Milo's mood, but he hadn't given her the opportunity. Now he'd disappeared, leaving her at a loose end. She didn't want to read, couldn't use her laptop for fear of her activities being monitored, and the thought of watching daytime television made her want to scream. She could go out for a walk, she supposed—there was a pretty park nearby—but it was too hot to bother.

She followed Milo's advice, wandered out onto the terrace, and threw herself full length onto a well-upholstered chaise, the size of a double bed. She continued to brood about Milo, reminding herself just how delectable he'd looked when he had arrived home in his business suit. If the magistrate had been a lady, no matter how old, her decision would have had to be influenced by having such an Adonis standing before her, pleading for his client—no question. She should have asked him how it had gone, but his closed expression hadn't exactly invited conversation. It was as though he was pissed at her for some reason, but she couldn't think what had changed since yesterday.

It would make her life so much easier if having gone to bed with him had gotten her over her obsession. Unfortunately the reverse was true, especially now she'd seen his scars, knew how vulnerable they made him feel, and had learned from Hal how they came to be there. That revelation left her with a bigger problem—one she didn't have a clue how to go about resolving.

Milo and Hal would have to know, sooner or later, that she'd agreed to go to Pakistan with a group of like-minded volunteers to help with the refugee crisis in situ. There were never enough helpers, and she looked forward to making a real difference. That's what she had wanted to check online for news about. There was a website with regular updates. Still, she would receive an e-mail when the arrangements were completed. Anyway, she couldn't leave the country until after this debacle was resolved and her passport was returned to her, so perhaps Milo and Hal wouldn't need to know.

Jodie shivered, in spite of the warmth, when she considered their reaction—especially Milo's—should they find out. How could she make them understand she wasn't just playing at this? There was a force within her that stirred her compassion, leaving her with no choice but to follow her conscience. They seemed to think it was a deliberate ploy to upset her father, to get back at him in some way for neglecting her. Perhaps it had started out that way, but now, helping these displaced people was her *raison d'être.* It gave her life purpose and meaning, and she absolutely believed what she was doing was right. Milo and Hal had seen these war zones through the eyes of soldiers, risking their lives for political causes that might not always have seemed clear to them. She could quite see that, and understand their position.

Why couldn't they understand hers?

The sun was tempered by a slight breeze coming off the river. Even so, its rays soaked into Jodie's skin, making her drowsy. She fell into a semi-sleep, dreaming of Milo's skilled hands bringing her body alive, of his terrible scars, and how they had come about, of her father, who had at last noticed her, but for all the wrong reasons. Damn it, this had been a lovely dream, until her father intruded. She closed off images of him, aware of the liquid oozing out of her as she relived her time in Milo's bedroom. Jodie let out a needy little sigh, wondering if Milo's distant attitude meant no action replay would be forthcoming.

Damn it, why was he sending her so many mixed messages? She ticked off the confusing signals on her fingers, wondering what she was supposed to make of them. He didn't shower with his bed partners, yet he had showered with her. He didn't reveal his scars to anyone, and yet he'd allowed her to touch them when she washed his body. He didn't sleep all night with the women he played with, and yet he'd slept like a baby with her head resting on his chest.

Now he hardly wanted to speak to her.

Men!

She didn't think she'd fallen completely asleep, but must have done. She was woken by a firm hand shaking her shoulders.

"Jodie, wake up."

"Hmm." She blinked, drowsy and disorientated, unable to scc much because the sun was right overhead. "What is it?"

Milo crouched in front of her chaise, waving his cell phone beneath her nose. "Your dad," he said softly. "He's heard about the photograph, I'm afraid. One of the big papers contacted him."

"Oh, shit! Bet he's not too happy."

Milo's lips twitched. "I think he's had better days. He just tore me a new one for letting it happen."

"You weren't even there."

"Don't sweat it. I'm a big boy and can give as good as I get. He's on hold, wants to talk to you. Are you up to that?"

"No, but he won't give up until he's yelled at me as well." Jodie sighed as she reached her hand out for the phone. "Let's get it over with."

"Press that green button."

As he handed over the phone, their fingers clashed. Jodie widened her eyes, blown away by the charge that spiraled through her at the simple contact. She glanced up at Milo and could tell from his expression, his look of black surprise, he felt it, too. He didn't waste time examining his feelings, but quickly stepped away from her, the coward! Jodie thought he would make a swift exit and give her some privacy. To her surprise, he took a seat opposite her chaise and sent her a brief, yet devastating smile. It was like he was battling with himself. He didn't want to stay, but thought she needed protecting from the man on the other end of the phone, who was thousands of miles away and had long ago lost the ability to control her. The better she got to know this annoyingly complex, intelligent, drop-dead gorgeous Brit, the less she understood him.

Sighing, Jodie took a deep breath and pressed the green button.

"Hey, Dad."

"Jodie, what the devil's going on over there? I've told Hanson I don't want him looking out for you. The man's obviously incompetent."

I'm fine thanks, Dad. How are you? "I'm happy with Milo, thanks."

"Which tells me all I need to know about your judgment. Do you realize what's happening over here now this story's gotten out? Do you have any idea what you've done?"

Jodie wasn't sure what she was supposed to say to that, so she said nothing, letting him rant on, hoping he'd get it out of his system. When that showed no signs of happening, something inside her snapped.

"Sorry, Dad, you're breaking up. Must be a bad signal. I can't hear a word you're saying." She chanced a brief glance at Milo, astonished to find him sending her a full-wattage, non-contrived smile. At last she'd gotten through to him, even if he was just sympathizing over her dad. Not that it mattered. Pathetic creature that she was, she'd take what she could get of him. "No, sorry, I didn't get that, either." She stifled a giggle when Milo placed his hands over his ears, implying he could hear her father yelling when the phone wasn't even on speaker. "I'm gonna have to call you back. Bye."

She ended the called and expelled another deep sigh. Dealing with her father was exhausting at the best of times. When he was mad at her, it was completely impossible. He had only ever cared about number one, and nothing had changed in that respect. She caught Milo's gaze focused on her face, serious and concerned. To her utter astonishment, she then saw the funny side of the situation, and laughed aloud. Instead of carting her off to the funny farm, Milo laughed too, a deep, rich belly laugh, which is when Jodie really lost it. She laughed until she cried, tears streaming down her face, probably making her eyes look blotchy and unattractive, but still she was unable to stop.

It was cathartic, and when she finally managed to get control of herself she felt a whole lot better. So what if Milo didn't want her anymore? So what if she'd been accused of being a terrorist? So what if she'd messed up her dad's career? No one had died, the world continued to spin, and—best of all—she hadn't given in to her father's bully-boy tactics.

"Sorry," she said, wiping her eyes with the back of her hand. "But if you could have heard him—"

"I did. So did half of Battersea, I would imagine."

"He's not a happy bunny," Jodie said, sobering. "His language wasn't at all senatorial, but I suppose I can't blame him for that."

"Sounded like he's got a poker stuck up his arse."

Jodie agreed. "How did the press get onto him so quickly?" she asked. "That picture was only taken a couple of hours ago."

"Ah, the wonders of the Internet age. Once the connection was made to your father it was always going to be a big story. Especially at this time of year. August is a slow news month."

"Oh."

She expected Milo to leave her again. He didn't. Instead he remained where he was, focusing a deep, penetrating gaze upon her face, his own expression dark, unreadable. The only sound was the traffic in the street several floors below them, and a radio playing softly in a nearby apartment. Jodie was still miffed by his earlier treatment of her, and wanted to be the one to get up and walk out this time.

She didn't move. She couldn't seem to find the will. Instead their gazes locked, and held. She drowned in the depths of his beautiful gray eyes, willing the moment to last indefinitely. She ought to say something to defuse the situation, assure him she expected nothing more from him. *Liar!* Words were beyond her. God, she loved him! Even more than she had for the past ten years now she knew he was less than perfect, physically and mentally. She moistened her lips, and he groaned. But still he didn't speak. Sexual tension fuelled the atmosphere, and it was that which finally galvanized Jodie into action.

"What do you want from me?" she asked quietly.

"What do you mean?"

"Don't play games, Milo Hanson," she replied, getting annoyed. "You know very well you're sending me mixed messages, and I want to know why. I think you owe me that much."

"You're very beautiful when you get mad. Your eyes burn like a raging bush fire. Has anyone ever told you that?"

Jodie sprang to her feet. "Don't you dare patronize me!"

"I wasn't. Believe it or not, I was trying to pay you a compliment." A smile tugged at his sculpted lips. "You're supposed to thank me. It's polite."

She snarled at him with her face averted, unable to meet his heavy-lidded, seductive gaze for fear of revealing her deep desire for him. When he looked like he did right now, a little boy lost, sad, and confused, her feelings for him went off the chart. "What would you know about polite?" she asked petulantly.

"I'm trying here, Jodie," he said, his voice sounding strained as he dropped his head into his splayed hands and shook it from side to side. "Really trying."

"Is that what you do with all your conquests? Have your wicked way with them, then don't want to know."

His head shot up. "That's not fair."

She sent him a challenging glare. "Isn't it?"

"Hal told you, didn't he?" he asked after a prolonged, heated pause. "About my leg."

"Yes."

"Then you know what's wrong with me, if anything's wrong."

"Because I want to help refugees?" She tossed her head, wishing he'd stand up so she could batter his chest with her fists. Something, anything to relieve the growing frustration swelling inside her. "You, Hal, and I aren't joined at the hip, Milo. This is for now, not forever. Live for the moment, or tell me to go to a hotel." She folded her arms and turned away from him. "I can't handle the cold shoulder, nor do I deserve it. You're supposed to be on my side."

She walked the length of the terrace, as far away from him as she could get. Jodie stared out at the river, hugging her arms across her torso, willing the tears that had sprung to her eyes not to fall. She'd been wrong about Milo. Wrong to spend all these years lusting after him. He wasn't worth it.

She didn't hear him stand up. Hal was right—he was as smooth and silent as a panther when it suited his purpose. The first time she realized he'd approached her was when his arms slid around her waist from behind, covering her own. She gasped, and tried to struggle out of his grasp. Not that she tried all that hard. Anyway, she never would have managed it. He was way too strong for her and, anyway, her insides went into free fall the moment he touched her, making escape out of the question.

"Sorry," he said, nuzzling her hair with his lips. "I'm a jackass sometimes."

"No arguments from me on that one."

"Forgive me, baby."

He turned her in his arms and transferred his lips from her hair to her mouth. Jodie didn't care if she seemed like a pushover—she simply couldn't resist him when he displayed his neuroses. His arms slid around her neck, playing with her collar. She parted her lips, allowing his tongue free access to her mouth, and could feel the full and impressive extent of his erection pressing against her belly. She managed to expel a needy little moan around their kiss, emptied her mind of her grievances, and simply kissed him back.

"Come on," he said, breaking the kiss far too soon for Jodie's liking.

He took her hand and led her to the chaise she'd been resting on earlier. Now she understood why it was so large. Presumably he made a habit out of bringing his women here to admire the view. She quelled the jealousy this thought engendered, took her own advice, and lived for the moment.

Sitting down, he pulled her into his lap. She leaned her head against his shoulder, wondering where this was leading—hoping she knew.

"You're the first woman ever to see what happened to me. Did Hal tell you that?"

"Yes, he did. That's why I didn't understand—"

"Jodie, I never should have started this." He shook his head. "I'm your solicitor, your lawyer, or whatever. It's not professional."

She bit her lip in an effort to hold back a smile. "I won't tell if you don't."

"Even so."

"Then why did you? Start it, I mean. Invite me to stay here. It was obvious you didn't like me, or what I stood for, when you came to the police station, so why inflict yourself with me?"

He ran a hand through his hair. "I couldn't seem to help myself." He emitted a hollow laugh. "I think I must have a death wish, or something."

"Because our views differ?" She widened her eyes, unable to understand why it should matter to him so much, in spite of his disfigured leg. It wasn't as if she was staying indefinitely. "I know you've seen more horrible things than I could ever imagine. I know you have good reason not to trust displaced people, and you think I'm hopeless naïve, but—"

He placed a finger against her lips to shut her up. "All of those reasons," he replied. "I don't usually look into a woman's politics if I'm attracted to her, but there's something different about you." His voice was a soft, persuasive purr that vibrated through her body, sending delicious desire rioting through her bloodstream. His eyes, dark and intense, shimmered with hot intentions. "And I want you so much it hurts worse than my fucking leg ever did."

Jodie moistened her lips with the tip of her tongue and sent him a sexy, challenging smile. "Then quit talking and do something about it."

Chapter Eleven

Milo shook his head in response to Jodie's challenge. Even if he wasn't competitive by nature, it would have been beyond him to reject it. He felt something inside of him erupt when their gazes collided, as though a hidden part of him had been released from a cage. Desire waged war against common sense, a one-sided battle that was over before it even began. Milo reminded himself not to overthink the situation, and go with his instincts.

Carpe diem.

"I guess Daddy already wants to fire me," he said, brushing the hair away from Jodie's forehead, and planting a kiss on the bridge of her freckled nose. "Might as well live down to his expectations."

"I want another lesson, Milo." She reached up and tangled her fingers in his hair, tugging at it, her expression a combination of resolution and desperation. "What you and Hal did to me last night, what Hal did to me this morning, changed something inside me." She blinked eyes that burned with passion. "It's as though I'm just finding out who I'm supposed to be."

"You like being given orders?"

"Yeah." She laughed self-consciously. "Who would have thought it? I don't usually take well to authority, to being told what to do."

Milo laughed. "I guess your daddy's finding that out for himself."

"It's a bit late for him to play the part of the caring parent." She wrinkled her pert little nose. "Half the time while I was growing up, I think he forgot he even had a daughter."

Milo came from a close, perfectly normal family, so didn't feel qualified to comment.

"It's not uncommon for people in our scene to act completely out of character, once they put the day job behind them and stop behaving the way the world thinks they should," he said instead. "That's why people go to BDSM clubs. They're in an arena where no one will judge them because everyone is there for similar, hedonistic reasons that to the outside world might seem warped or twisted. Highly intelligent captains of industry can be found cleaning the floor with a toothbrush held between their teeth, or having a Dominatrix walking over their chests in five-inch spiked heels, stuff like that."

"Yin and yang?" Jodie frowned. "The clever guys need to cede their responsibilities for a while, and live out their fantasies."

"Precisely. We all have alter egos that need airing occasionally." He canted his head and fixed her with a penetrating look. "So, what's your fantasy, darling? What do you lie in bed of a night, dreaming about?"

She choked on a gurgle of laughter. "I couldn't possibly tell you that."

"Oh, but that's the whole point of this game. You become someone else. You're no longer Jodie Bisset, American vigilante, but—"

"Is that how you see me? As a vigilante."

"Poor choice of words," he muttered in a velvety-smooth tone. "It doesn't matter what makes you tic on the outside world. The whole point of these games is to release our inner gods or goddesses, and be whatever we damned well want to be for a while."

"Well, I like you telling me what to do. I like you tying me up. I liked it when you spanked me." Her face flooded with color, but her gaze collided with his, and didn't budge. Sincerity and mild surprise, presumably at her candor, formed the bedrock of her expression. Milo was particularly pleased to have awakened her curiosity. He'd put her on the path to who she was supposed to be, and tried not to resent the fact that he wouldn't always be on hand to see her flourish in her newfound role as an obedient little sub. "There, I've said it."

"That's real good, babe. Half the battle is accepting what you want, and not being afraid to go after it."

Milo tipped her off his lap and she fell onto her back on the chaise with a startled *oh*, laughing and breathless, her faced flushed.

"Stay there," Milo said, resisting the urge to ravish her then and there. Somehow. "Don't move a muscle, I'll be right back."

Her eyes widened. "You're going to fuck me out here, in the open."

Milo's chuckle sounded decidedly wicked, even to his own ears. "You got something against fresh air?"

"People might see us."

"And that would bother you because…"

"Absolutely." She nodded vigorously, but the gleam in her eyes gave her away. The prospect turned her on.

"Don't worry, babe. I don't want anyone to see you come for me. That's private." He sent her a carnal smile. "That won't happen. We're not overlooked, unless someone going past on a boat happens to have binoculars trained on us. Course, if anyone below us has their windows open, I can't promise they won't hear your screams." He winked at her. "Or you begging to be fucked."

"Milo!"

He chuckled, went to his room to fetch what he needed, and returned to the terrace clutching the props he'd gone to collect. Jodie was right where he'd left her, on her back, an enigmatic smile flirting with her lips, pert nipples pressing against the fabric of her top. She was so goddamned beautiful, so wanton, so every damned thing, he was unsure if he could actually go through with this, and remain detached. It wouldn't be enough. He would never want to let her go. Shit, what was she doing to him?

Milo took a moment to segue into his role as Dom. He leaned against the railing, and fixed her with a stern expression that immediately caused her to drop her gaze. Without being told to, she sat up, cross-legged, hands resting neatly on her thighs.

"Stand up and take your jeans and top off," Milo said brusquely.

She was clumsy in her haste to comply, and it took her two attempts to get up from the chaise. Milo remained where he was, making no effort to help her. She pulled her top over her head and threw it aside, briefly raising her eyes to him, presumably to see if he approved. Did he approve? Shit, she was smoking hot today in a lacy blue bra that struggled to contain her full tits. They spilled over the top of the cups as though they couldn't wait to get the show on the road. Milo empathized.

He hissed at Jodie, she got the message, and immediately lowered her eyes again. No one could say she wasn't a quick study. More slowly this time, she unsnapped her jeans and jerked down the zip. She pulled the denim down her legs, sitting on the edge of the chaise so she could step out of her pants completely. Then she stood again, and did that thing with folding her hands across her pussy. They failed to hide her matching panties—no, make that a thong—which barely covered her pubic hair. Milo was on fire, unable to suppress a groan. He picked up a pillow from another chair and threw it at Jodie's feet.

"Kneel on that, and rest your torso over the chaise," he ordered curtly.

She moistened her lips, trembling as she did as he asked. Her butt was now stuck in the air, exposed for his pleasure, covered with just the string of her thong separating her firm, lean buttocks. He would leave it there, for now. Having given way to temptation, Milo had no intention of rushing things.

"Have you behaved yourself today, Jodie?" he asked in a severe tone.

"No, Sir." Her voice was muffled against the cushions of the chaise. "I let those photographers take my picture. And I was rude to my dad on the phone."

"What does that mean?"

"It means I must be punished."

"Then ask me."

"Please, Master, punish me for letting you down."

"How would you like to be punished, darling?"

"However it would please you to punish me, Master."

Christ, she couldn't possibly know what she was saying!

"I have a leather riding crop here." He smacked it against the palm of his hand, and she flinched. "I'm going to use it on your backside, teach you a lesson. How many strokes do you think you deserve?"

"I…I'm not sure."

"Remember the safe words," he said, bringing the crop down lightly over her buttocks.

She flinched and cried out, but whether in shock, pain, or pleasure it was hard to say. She didn't use the safe words, so if it was pain she must have found it endurable. He hadn't touched her, prepared her in any way like he did the last time, and wondered if perhaps he should have done. She was still so new to this, even if she had taken to it like a natural.

Overthinking again, Hanson. He repeated the process, a little harder, and this time she didn't make a sound. That was good. Four more strikes, and he figured she would have had enough, for now.

"Do you have something to say to me, Jodie?"

"Yes, Sir. Thank you for chastising me."

"You're very welcome, baby."

He sat on the edge of the chaise, shirtless but still wearing his jeans, and bent to examine her backside.

"You have pretty pink stripes across your arse," he said. "Very becoming."

He placed a hand on her left buttock and softly caressed it with bold sweeps of his palm. She mumbled something incoherent. Milo bent his head and kissed the area he'd just beaten, his lips firm but gentle, his tongue washing away the hurt.

"Spanking you really turns me on, baby," he said softly.

"Me too," she replied into the cushions.

"Hmm, is that so?" He slid a finger inside her panties, unsurprised to discover that they were soaked through. "Yep, it obviously does." He chuckled, sliding that finger deep into her cunt.

Jodie groaned, and pushed back against his digit. Milo immediately withdrew it, causing her to smother a complaint.

"Keep absolutely still, darling," he said, leaning over her back to trail a line of damp kisses down her spine. She shivered, clearly not happy about remaining passive. "This won't do," he said, standing up to retrieve the handcuffs he'd brought with him. "You have to learn to take orders, or suffer the consequences. Lie flat on your belly," he ordered.

* * * *

The small part of Jodie's brain still capable of rational thought wondered if she'd lost her mind. She was practically naked on a balcony in broad daylight, and had just allowed a man she barely knew to beat the living crap out of her with a riding crop. It had stung like the devil, but she'd loved every minute of it, especially when she glanced sideways from beneath the hair cascading over her face and saw the extent of Milo's erection testing the strength of his zipper.

What did he intend to do to her now, she wondered, as she stood up, stiff from kneeling for so long. She sank down onto the soft cushions of the chaise again, on her front, as instructed. Whatever it was, she was happy to play along, just so long as he took her bra off. Her nipples were rock solid, and the abrasive lace cups were cutting painfully into them. God, but she loved this complex man, demons notwithstanding! And she would do whatever it took to make him happy, no matter the discomfort to her. Not that she was uncomfortable, precisely, just falling apart with desire and excitement—desperate to have that glorious cock of his buried deep inside her.

"Lift your arms out above your head."

Was he going to shackle her hands? She felt first one fluffy restraint and then the other snap around her wrists. Part of her was disappointed. She had so wanted to explore that lovely chest of his, but she already knew he didn't like to be touched because of...well, because of the unimaginable things that had happened to him that had left him permanently damaged. Still, at least she could peep up at him, get the occasional glimpse when he didn't realize she was looking.

Something was placed over her eyes and her world went dark. Shit, he'd blindfolded her. So much for breaking the rules. Was he a mind reader now?

"Take your weight on your elbows and forearms."

She did so and sensed the cuffs being attached to something in front of her. She had a limited range of movement available to her so would have to keep still. It would be very uncomfortable if she shifted her weight off of her elbows which was, presumably, the point.

"Up on your knees," he said curtly.

"Yes, Sir."

"Are you comfortable?" he asked when she complied.

"My nipples are painful inside this bra, Master."

He chuckled. "Well, we wouldn't want that."

Jodie waited for her bra to fall away. It didn't happen. Instead, Milo's large, oh-so-capable hands reached beneath her and pulled each of her breasts out of the cups of her bra, leaving them wedged above them, just as they'd had her do the previous day.

"Better?" he asked.

"Hmm."

He slid beneath her, sideways on, and alternately suckled and nipped at one of her hard nipples. The fingers of one hand plucked at the other one, pinching it hard, pulling it away from her body, elongating it. This was more painful, more intoxicatingly erotic, than the beating she'd just taken. Oh, what she would give for the use of her hands, or just one glimpse of his expression!

Just when she felt on the point of self-combustion, Milo abandoned her breasts. One hand grasped her jaw as he slid his index finger across her lips, tapping them with it. She opened up and sucked it deep inside. He groaned, thrusting it in and out of her mouth, mirroring the action she hoped he would soon take with his cock. Her pussy was dripping, thrumming with need. This torture was…well, torturous. Milo removed his finger from her mouth, and licked his way along her jaw. His tongue reached her neck, his gentleness as arousing as the force with which he'd just spanked her. Yin and yang, she reminded herself as, without warning, he grabbed the back of her collar and yanked her head backward, cutting off her air supply. Just for a moment she panicked. She couldn't breathe, but the heady feeling of floating outside of herself was too awesome for her to care. The blood pounded through her ears, she felt dizzy, and then, suddenly, she could breathe again.

"You like that?"

"Yes," she gasped, still panting to get enough air back in her lungs.

"It feels more intense because you can't see, can't anticipate what I'm going to do to you next, and because you can't use your hands," he said in the soft, mesmerizing, yet authoritative voice she could listen to all day. "It means you have to trust me because you're at my complete mercy. You're almost naked, in the open air, and you have no idea what I have planned for you. Does that excite you, Jodie?"

"Yes, Sir." She felt ashamed of her own desperation, and her inability to conceal it from him. "Very much."

"Course, I have some calls to make. I might have to leave you here like this for a while. Come back and finish what I started later."

"No!" Jodie was almost crying with disappointment. "Please, don't go!"

"Well, if you're *that* desperate. Perhaps I'll stay for a while and teach you some self-control."

When? Does that mean we'll do this again? Please say it does.

"If you continue to behave, at dinner tonight, we might very well make you assume this position in the corner while Hal and I eat."

Jodie gasped—with excitement. Why did the thought of being humiliated turn her on so comprehensively? Milo heard her reaction, of course, and chuckled, seemingly pleased with her response. She sensed him sliding out from beneath her, and resuming his position behind. Without warning his hand came down over her ass, hard. She flinched, but held her position on her bent arms, absorbing the unexpected pain, waiting for the tingling sensation to flush through her. She steeled herself for a second blow, which didn't come. Instead she felt the string of her thong being pulled away and something cool trickling between her buttocks.

"Lube," he said softly, rubbing it in with slow, deliberate fingers. "Need to get you used to the idea of having your sweet arse fucked."

Jodie's breathing quickened. Was that what she wanted? Hell, yes, if it would please Milo she would put up with anything, no matter how uncomfortable! His slick finger circled her anus and she instinctively tensed up.

"Shush, it's okay." She felt his hair tickle her buttocks, then his breath peppering them. "Just trust me, sugar, and let me in."

His other hand slid beneath her, inside her panties, and touched her swollen clit. The pleasure she felt was as unexpected as it was distracting. Desire consumed her and she forgot all about his finger playing with her backside, until she felt it slide past her tight coil of muscle, straight inside. The sensation was unbelievable, beyond anything she would have imagined possible, and she cried out with a combination of shock and pleasure.

"Yes," he said in that appreciative purr of his that so got to her. "And it gets way better than that. Just trust me."

He removed his finger with a soft plopping sound, but she felt it being replaced by something unfamiliar.

"A butt plug," he whispered. "To distend you. Let me slide it in, darling. It will blow your mind."

By that point, Jodie would have let him do anything he wanted. She was literally panting with need, her body bathed in perspiration, hot electrical signals flying between her synapses and setting her entire nervous system alight. The plug slid into her more easily than she would have anticipated, feeling alien yet not unpleasant. Milo's fingers pushed it a little deeper, and it settled into her like a gift from heaven.

"You see," he said, leaning over her to kiss her shoulder. "You're a natural at this."

Jodie wanted to ask what happened next. She desperately needed to be fucked, but how could they when she had the plug in her backside? Surely he didn't mean to remove it and replace it with his cock?

"It's okay, baby," he murmured, presumably because he sensed her momentary panic. "I won't do anything to you you don't like."

She felt him leave the chaise, and heard the sound of a zipper. He was back behind her again in seconds, his solid erection pushing against her butt. The sound of a foil packet ripping open made her heart sing with relief. She didn't care which orifice he chose for his cock, just so long as he buried it deep, and fucked her hard. Jodie was in no mood to be treated gently.

Without warning, he pulled her panties aside and, with the plug still inserted in her anus, thrust into her slick cunt from behind with one hard jerk of his hips.

"Oh!"

"I'm hurting you?"

"No, but I feel like I'm going to burst, with you and the plug thingy."

The sound of Milo's rich, throaty laughter filled her with joy. "Not a chance. You'll get used to it, and then you'll wonder how you ever lived without it."

"Perhaps."

Milo, buried ball-deep inside her, stopped moving. "Do you want me to fuck you, Jodie?"

"Yes, God yes!"

"Then you'd best ask me nicely."

"Please, Milo, I've waited ten years for this moment."

She felt his body tense. "You've what!"

Shit, did she say that aloud? "Just fuck me, please!"

"Now that," he said, a smile in his voice, "I can do."

He gyrated his hips, his cock pushing so deep that it felt as though the plug would slide out of her. Something would have to give—there wasn't enough room for both. She felt gloriously and completely full, ready to fly without wings.

They groaned in unison as Milo set a hot, slick tempo, sliding in and out of her with a precise skill that fired her blood and stunned her senses. Oh, what she would give to be able to see him, to touch him. He was fucking her from behind again, even though she was blindfolded and she couldn't see his scars. He really did have a hang-up about them. She wanted to tell him there was no need, but didn't have the breath to spare. Besides, she wasn't allowed to speak unless spoken to. *Oh, Milo, my beautiful, damaged Milo!*

"Stay with me, darling. This is gonna get rough."

"Yes, I'll always be with you." *I always have been.*

His rhythm stuttered. Shit, she'd spoken out of turn again, giving too much away about her feelings for him. He wasn't just messing with the self-control wielded over her desires, but appeared to have invaded her mind, too. Jodie no longer seemed capable of thinking before she spoke.

"Good to know," he said, picking up the pace again.

Jodie's limbs trembled as she worked with him, pushing back to meet his thrusts, encouraging him to go as deep as he could get, but it never felt deep enough to exorcise the longing she had harbored for so long for this beautiful man. She would never get enough of Milo Hanson. If he went through another mercurial mood swing, she might never have even this much of him again, so she intended to make the most of his full and complete attention. His body—his beautiful muscular body—covered hers from behind, hot and needy, as he worked her pussy in a punishing rhythm. She could feel his cock expand inside of her, and knew he had to be close. She would have liked to test the extent of his control, but it was too late for that. She felt the familiar coiling in her gut, and her desire spiraled beyond her control. Her pussy tightened, muscles clenching, and she couldn't hold it.

"Milo, I can't…I'm going to come, I'm sorry, I—"

"It's okay, darling, take what you need." The severity of his thrusting increased in time with his heavy breathing. "Come for me, Jodie. Let it all go, darling."

He thrust into her harder than ever, pulling at a solidified nipple harshly with the fingers of one hand, which was all it took. The heated passion behind his words, the feel of his thick cock overfilling her, caused her world to fragment.

"Holy shit, Milo. Just fuck me!"

Head flung back, senses heightened by her lack of vision, Jodie clung greedily to his cock, closing her muscles around it as her body went into spasm. Delicious shivers radiated from her core, reverberating like thunder through her midsection, and spreading to the outermost reaches of her body on a surging tide of pleasure. Her blood ignited, running like molten lava through her veins as she satiated her ravenous hunger.

For now, at least.

Milo stilled just long enough for her to detonate around him. Then, swatting her rear hard as he increased the force of his thrusts, he too toppled over the edge of a bottomless abyss.

"Oh, sweet Jodie!" They fell onto their sides, still joined together, breathing hard. "You never fail to amaze me."

Chapter Twelve

"Hey, guys, I'm back."

No answer. The main room in the loft was empty, no sign of Milo anywhere. He'd been in a strange mood before Hal went out, so he'd probably taken himself off somewhere to avoid Jodie. They needed to talk about that. Milo acting so out of character, not appearing to know his own mind, was unusual enough to be concerning.

Where *was* Jodie? Hal hoped she hadn't argued with Milo and been the one to storm off. She was a bit of a firebrand, particularly where Milo was concerned, and he wouldn't put it past her to do something that impetuous.

Sighing, Hal glanced out at the terrace, and did a double-take.

"Well, well," he said, grinning broadly. "I didn't see that one coming, pun intended."

He stepped up to the door and watched the show. They were so into one another that Milo and Jodie hadn't heard Hal arrive home. He leaned against the doorframe, watching Milo fuck Jodie's brains out, still grinning inanely.

"Not interrupting anything, am I?" he asked when Milo, grunting and swearing, finally let himself go.

Milo laughed, leaned over to kiss Jodie's shoulder, removed her blindfold, and withdrew from her.

"Make yourself useful, and release Jodie from those cuffs while I deal with this condom."

Milo stood up, grabbed his scattered clothing, and sauntered off, looking pretty damned pleased with himself.

"Hey, babe." Hal took the place on the chaise that Milo had just vacated and leaned over to release the handcuffs.

Jodie sat up and rubbed at her wrists. "Hey, yourself," she said. "What news of my friends."

"Nothing specific." Hal needed to talk to Milo about what he'd learned before he shared. "You and Milo looked like you were having fun."

She laughed self-consciously. "I've turned into a nymphomaniac since moving in with you guys."

Hal grinned. "That's my favorite type of nymph."

"Right. And what other types do you know?"

"Well, let me see. There's nympholepsy."

She blinked. "Pardon?"

"There's no need to look so surprised. Milo isn't the only one with brains in this set-up."

"Okay, so what does it mean?"

"Passion aroused in men by beautiful females." He ran a finger slowly down her arm, fixing her with an intense look. "It's what you do to me, babe. And Milo, judging by the show you guys just put on."

"Thank you for saying that." She placed a chaste kiss on his cheek. "It's so sweet."

It was hot on the terrace, with full-on sun now directly overhead. Hal pulled his shirt over his head and threw it aside. Jodie glanced at his chest, licked her lips, and smiled her approval. She shifted her position, as though wanting to get close enough to touch him, and then winced.

"Are you hurt, darling? Did Milo spank you too hard?"

"No, it's not that." Jodie blushed scarlet. "But he…er, forgot to remove something."

Hal cupped her face with the fingers of one hand, grinning. "I doubt that. Milo doesn't forget things. Butt plug, huh?"

"Hmm."

"Is it uncomfortable?"

"Well no, but—"

"It will distend you, darling. For later."

She blinked. "Later? How long do I have to keep this thing inside me?"

"I expect he has plans."

She tossed her head, but her irritation looked contrived. "Nice of him to share them."

"We're in charge, remember."

"True, but I'm not sure about this."

"Ask him when he comes back. But never forget, you don't have to do anything you don't want to."

"I will ask, and not just about that."

"You look like you have something on your mind." Hal touched her cheek gently with his fingertips. "Care to share?"

She shrugged. "It's Milo, he's so full of contradictions. I still don't get where he's coming from, what he wants from me." She stifled a giggle. "Other than the obvious. It's exhausting trying to keep up with his mercurial moods."

Hal chuckled. "Join the club. Milo has a tendency to overthink every situation."

"Oh, so I'm a situation now, am I?"

"Hey, don't get mad at me." Hal pushed his hands toward her, palms out. "If it's any consolation, I've never seen him like this before. You've gotten under his skin, babe."

Jodie tossed her head. "Is that supposed to make me feel better?"

"Just telling it like it is."

"Well, I like you way better than I like him."

Hal laughed. "That won't work, darling. Milo and I are a team—a package deal. We won't let you play favorites."

"I still don't get how that came about. I mean, no offence, but you're different animals."

"We come from different walks of life, it's true, but the service is a great leveler. Once we got over hating each other—I thought he was so far up himself he needed a flashlight to find his way, he thought I was a mindless thug—we hit it off. He saved me from that quicksand, and…"

"And what did you save him from?" Jodie asked when Hal's words stalled.

"A predatory woman."

Jodie raised both brows. "He didn't know how to fend off women without help?"

"The women that hang around the SAS headquarters in Hereford are a rare and determined breed, not for the fainthearted." Hal shuddered, making her laugh. "Trust me on this."

"Milo's no wimp."

"No, but he was a bit naïve back then. I, on the other hand, graduated from the backstreets of east London. You don't survive that school of knocks without learning just about every trick in the book, not to mention writing half of them yourself. Milo was right about me. I *was* a thug before I joined the army." He laughed. "Then it became all right, because I was getting paid to be violent. I channeled all the anger and aggression eating away at me into my career, stopped being so angry at the world, and quit trying to resolve every dispute with my fists. Probably saved me from a life behind bars," he added matter-of-factly.

"I'm sure it did."

"I had no education, dropped out of school before I was sixteen, and just kinda drifted for a while. Anyway, the army straightened me out, and while Milo was studying law in his ivory tower, I was working my way through the ranks."

"Then you applied for the SAS and met Milo."

"Right, and the women who hang out around Hereford know what they want. We're supposed to be the toughest of the tough, the elite, and women go for all that macho bullshit. It's why we volunteer, of course."

Jodie punched his arm. "Be serious!"

"Perhaps I was." Hal blew her a kiss. "Those women at Hereford, I gotta tell you, their jungle telegraph is more efficient than any communication system the army's come up with. They knew all about Milo before he stepped off the bus. Looks, brains, money, and a tough guy. What was not to like? Needless to say, he was swamped, and he picked up with a real classy babe. It got quite heavy. Too heavy for Milo, and he backed off, making excuses not to see her. So she upped and told him she was pregnant."

"Ah, and was she?"

"Milo, the trusting fool, didn't even think to ask that question. But, like you, it was the first thing that occurred to me when I came across him crying into his beer, and he told me what had happened. He liked the woman, but didn't love her, and definitely didn't want to get married. But, you know, his kid, and all. He felt he had no choice."

"You had your doubts about the woman?"

"I did a little digging. Watched her when she wasn't with Milo." Hal sighed. "It was a scam, I was sure of it, and I told Milo what I'd found. She shared a house with a guy, and although I couldn't prove it, I was willing to bet their relationship wasn't platonic. Anyway, I said to Milo to cool it with her. Tell her there was no hurry to marry. They could get hitched after the baby was born, and *after* they'd had a paternity test conducted. Needless to say, he never saw her again, Milo wised up, and we became best mates."

"That's quite a story."

"Yeah well, opposites attract. Milo had brains but I was the one with street smarts. We bonded, found out we liked the same sort of women, were both into BDSM and…well, when we left the service, Milo said I'd already proved myself as an investigator and we might as well stick together."

Jodie rested her head against Hal's shoulder and sighed. "That explains a lot."

"Sure, and there's more. Milo persuaded me to make up for lost education. I took courses in the army, read books Milo recommended, stuff like that. Learning as an adult, when you want to as opposed to having stuff forced on you as a kid, makes a big difference."

"And you feel you owe Milo for that?"

"Hell, no, we owe each other!"

Jodie laughed. "So you're a package deal, you say. Well, I've just had one half of the package. How about serving up the other half?"

She lifted her head from his shoulder and focused her gaze on his chest, the atmosphere between them taut with anticipation. The desire he detected swirling in the depths of her eyes reflected the way he felt. But Milo had just screwed her senseless, she still had the butt plug inside her, and he really shouldn't do what his cock was screaming at him to do.

"Probably not a good idea right now."

She pouted. "Don't you get all moody on me, too."

"Babe, given my way I'd fuck you every which way into the middle of next week. But you're not used to playing rough. Talking of which, that looks like it's cutting into you." Milo had pulled Jodie's tits out of the cups of her bra, and left them balancing over the top. Hal leaned forward and put them back where they belonged.

"Well, if that's the way you feel."

"Honey, you have no idea how I feel right now. I'm just thinking of you."

"Thanks, I think."

"It's just a rain check, as you Americans would say." Hal sent her a smoldering smile. "I shall definitely have my wicked way with you later. Count on it. I'm betting Milo will be up for an action replay, too."

"Talking of which, like I said earlier, I just don't understand your best *mate*." She scowled. "I thought he liked me after last night, and…well, you know. But today he was distant, almost rude, and went out of his way to avoid me. And now this." She gestured to the chaise. "I guess you two play with women all the time, and it's no big deal, but it's different for me. I'm selective, and don't usually do casual. Oh, don't get me wrong. It's not like I have unrealistic expectations," she added hastily, "but still…I don't know, spur of the moment is hard for me."

Hal took her hand and brushed his lips across her knuckles. "I'll talk to him, darling."

"No, don't do that. It doesn't matter. I don't want him to think I'm clinging like a vine." She pulled a wry face. "Besides, I practically had to talk him into this."

Hal very much doubted that. Jodie was a contradictory mix—full of self-confidence, determination, brash even, when it came to the defense of her *causes*—insecure, and out of her depth when it came to Milo and him.

She had that just-fucked glow in her eye, still had Milo's butt plug buried inside her, and that knowledge turned Hal on big time. Everything about her turned him on, especially the way she'd taken to playing their games like a natural. Hal placed a hand on either side of her face and moved in to kiss her, unable to resist, even if it could only lead to one thing. Hadn't he just decided she wasn't ready for more of the same yet?

Hal ignored his conscience, concentrating instead on plundering her mouth with his tongue, greedy and demanding. He sensed rather than heard Milo rejoin them. Sure enough, when he broke the kiss his buddy was leaning against the railings, watching them. His hair was damp, implying that he'd taken a quick shower. Barefoot and shirtless, he was wearing shorts—shorts that came down almost to his knees, covering his scars completely.

"Don't let me stop you," Milo said, looking amused.

"I was just saying *hi*. Jodie's just had you manhandling her. She needs a break."

"Doesn't Jodie have any say in the matter?" she asked, swiping her lower lip with the tip of her tongue as she shared a glance between them.

"No," they said together.

"I thought we'd take you out to dinner tonight," Milo said. "I'd suggest you get some rest first." He winked at her. "You'll need all your strength for later."

Dinner was news to Hal, but was probably a good idea. Get her out of the loft for a while, keep things in perspective. Jodie's face lit up.

"I'd like that."

"I forgot the plug." Milo nodded at Hal. "Wanna do the honors, bud?"

Hal shook his head, convinced Milo had deliberately *forgotten* it, just so Hal got to have his share of the fun. He probably thought he was being considerate, but what he was actually doing was testing Hal's limits a little too severely. She had a glorious arse, made for fucking. Hal's discomfort grew, along with his erection, but he ignored both.

"Turn over, darling," he said, shooting Milo a killer glare.

She flopped onto her belly, obligingly sticking her arse in the air. Christ! Hal couldn't resist running his hand across the smooth globes, still pink from where Milo must have spanked her. He dropped his head and kissed each in turn, before cutting to the chase. He had to do this, and do it quickly, otherwise his dwindling self-restraint would…well dwindle completely. He pulled the string of her thong aside, sucked his own finger to moisten it, and gently probed her anus. It was slick—probably a combination of lube and her own juices— and she barely flinched as his finger slid past her coiled muscle and found the end of the plug. He pulled gently and it slid out with a soft popping sound.

"All done," he said, tapping her arse lightly and replacing her thong.

"Thanks." She stood up and headed for the loft, not looking at either of them. "It's too hot out here. I'll go and rest in my room for a while."

"Good plan." Milo shared a bemused look with Hal. "Be ready to go out at seven."

"Yes, Sir," she replied curtly.

"What's her problem?" Milo asked as he and Hal also returned to the main room, and Hal cleaned and dried the plug at the kitchen sink.

"I guess she's confused, and she's not the only one." Hal leaned against the breakfast bar and focused his complete attention on Milo. "What's your take on her?"

Milo frowned. "What does it matter? She's only passing through."

"Don't bullshit me. You wouldn't have showered with her, and let her see your leg, if that's the way you feel."

"Yeah, you're right." Milo expelled a deep sigh, and ran a hand through his hair. "Okay, I'll admit it, she's got to me. I like her. A lot. Wish I didn't, it complicates everything, but there don't seem to be a whole lot I can do about it."

"There, that didn't hurt too much, did it?" Hal grinned at Milo, who scowled in response.

"It can't go anywhere. She's tied up with a whole bunch of stuff that I'd never feel comfortable with. It would only lead to fights, and...well—"

"Perhaps she'll give her causes up for us."

Milo flexed a brow. "You're thinking she's *the one*?"

"The possibility crossed my mind. I've never felt like this before."

"Me neither, but if you love someone, you don't ask them to give up their beliefs."

"Are we really talking *lurve* here?" Hal probably looked as surprised as he felt. "I mean, it's been less than two days."

"Hell if I know, mate. All I can tell you is I'd slay dragons for her, if that's what it takes. I'll go that extra mile to get her off those charges. Call in all the favors I need to, but what I can't do is sort her relationship with her old man. If you ask me, that's at the root of all her problems."

"And if she settled down with us," Hal added, serious for once, "she'd be giving up one controlling male in favor of two."

"The difference being we wouldn't try to make her live her life on our terms."

"Wouldn't we?" Hal raised a brow. "You just said you couldn't live with her *and* her causes."

Milo scowled. "Yeah, I did, didn't I?"

"She might be willing to come at them at a different, less dangerous, way." Hal took to pacing the length of the kitchen. "There has to be room for compromise."

"Perhaps." Milo threw his head back and let out a hollow laugh. "Why couldn't we have fallen for a boringly obedient little British girl with a safe nine-to-five job?"

Hal slapped Milo's shoulder. "Because we don't do boring, and we don't do nine to five, either."

"Yeah, there is that." Milo threw himself into a chair. "What did you learn in Camden Town?"

"I spoke with Phil and Betty at length. They were very subdued, and very pissed off at being arrested. They swore they knew nothing of Spectrum, and had no idea how those papers came to be in their house. They echoed what Jodie's already told us, and said loads of people are in and out all the time. Any one of them could have left the stuff there, and they would be none the wiser."

"Were there other people there today?"

"No, they said they wanted to keep to themselves until the arrest's been sorted, so they put the word out and their friends are staying away."

"Well, at least they're being sensible."

"They're scared shitless, Milo. I believed them when they said they knew nothing of Spectrum. They're just well-intentioned people, out of their depth."

Milo stretched his arms above his head, and yawned. "Did you press them on who might have left the papers?"

"Of course, but they weren't prepared to point the finger at anyone." Hal paused. "For what it's worth, if they had their suspicions, I think they would have told me, even if they didn't tell the police. They know this is heavy shit, and what will happen to them if they can't prove their innocence."

"Yeah well, maybe fear will concentrate their minds, and they'll think of something helpful."

"They actually asked me if you would represent them as well as Jodie."

Milo's head shot up. "They don't have their own representation?"

"Only legal aid. They don't have the funds for someone of your caliber."

"I can't take them on. Their interests could conflict with Jodie's."

"I know. I told them that, but said if anything came up in our investigation to clear Jodie, it would probably clear them, too."

"Right." Milo paused for a beat. "So, we're no farther forward, except we can forget about Phil and Betty being the guilty parties."

"Yeah, I'd stake my reputation on that."

"Okay, that's good enough for me."

Hal took the chair opposite Milo. "So, what now?"

Milo shrugged. "I guess we wait to see if any of the fingerprints on those documents match Jodie's. Unfortunately, I think they will."

"We can make a reasonable case for them being there if they do."

"Reasonable doubt might mean charges don't stick, but that won't help her old man's career. She'll be tainted by association, and so will he." Milo frowned. "Not that I give a shit about her father, but still, I can't see him taking a fall for his daughter's activities and not making her pay in some way."

"He sounds like a real piece of work," Hal said, grimacing.

"You got that right."

"Oh, I nearly forgot. One useful thing did come out of today. I showed Phil and Betty the picture I took of the photographers outside the nick, just on impulse, and they recognized one of them."

Milo jerked upright. "No shit! Do they know his name?"

"No, but they've seen him a few times hanging around near the house."

"With his camera?"

"No, but Betty said she saw him once in the local newsagents and, get this, she's adamant he spoke with an American accent."

"He's a Yank?" Milo probably looked as stunned as he felt. "Then how the fuck did he get a British press pass?"

"He might be a stringer for one of the big news agencies."

"Doubt it. We'd know him if he was." Milo scowled. "I don't like it. This doesn't smell right."

"You think one of her dad's political enemies arranged for those papers to be placed in the house?"

"I've always thought they were planted. Now I'm sure of it." Milo got up and headed for his study. "I'm gonna call Raoul and tell him we're looking for a Yank who's possibly based in the UK, maybe even in the US embassy."

"Fuck, this is big!"

"You said it, pal."

Chapter Thirteen

Jodie's mother's walk-in closet back in the States was larger than Jodie's entire London apartment. Perhaps that's why Jodie had taken an opposite stance, and traveled very light. Her London wardrobe—jeans, casual tops, comfortable, practical stuff—fit into a single suitcase. Today was the first time she'd regretted her lack of interest in clothes. She so wanted to look pretty and feminine for her dinner date with Milo and Hal. Given the lack of material she had to work with, that would be quite a challenge to pull off.

She lay in bed, tired, sore, hot from exposure from the sun but unable to sleep. For the first time since she couldn't remember when, she badly wanted to make an impression on a man—make that men. What she would give right now for access to her own collection of designer clothes, bought for her by her mother back in the States, most still with the labels intact.

Giving up on sleep, she got up, ran a bath, and poured a generous dollop of fragrant oil into the tub. Jodie eased herself into the steaming water, wincing as it covered her pussy and rather sore backside. Eyes closed, she lay back and though about Milo and Hal, still frustrated at her inability to read Milo. Hal, at least, was willing to talk about their shared history, but Milo's communication skills could use some work. Well, the verbal skills could, but there was nothing wrong with his actions. The moment he laid so much as one finger on her sensitized body, pathetic creature that she was, she became putty in his hands.

The same went for Hal. Okay, so she hadn't persuaded him to fuck her just now, but he'd wanted to, and was being considerate. Just thinking about the erotic way in which he'd removed the plug from her butt was enough to get her juices flowing. Jodie laughed. If she was turning into a slut, lusting after two men at the same time, she might as well enjoy the ride. She briefly thought about masturbating in the bath, anything to quell the near permanent state of arousal she'd been in since coming to lodge with the guys. She resisted, but only because she wanted to feel sexy and desirable tonight. That ambition would be easier to achieve if she didn't take the edge off her desire. She dunked her head beneath the water, and reached for the shampoo, telling herself to stop trying to second-guess Milo. She'd have fun with them tonight, treat it as casually as they did, and not think beyond that.

Jodie got out of the bath when the water started to cool, toweled herself dry, and then set about her hair. She found a dryer and, for once, took her time to style her wayward locks into a sleek curtain that tumbled halfway down her back. When she'd finished, at least her hair looked sophisticated, but her clothing…damn it, she wanted to look as sexy as the guys made her feel, and that would require a tight-fitting dress. But her meager wardrobe only allowed for two skirts, neither of which fit the bill.

She rummaged through her bag, and let out a small little cry of triumph when she came upon the very thing.

"I'd forgotten about you," she said to the pair of black satin, skintight pants she held in her hand. "You might just save the day."

She smiled to herself when she recalled the pants definitely didn't allow for anything to be worn beneath them. That would ruin the entire look. She pulled them on and critically examined the result in the full-length bathroom mirror, turning sideways, looking for telltale bulges. She couldn't see any.

"Hmm, not bad," she told her reflection.

The pants showed off her long legs well enough, but she needed high heels to finish the look. She only owned one pair. Hopefully Hal had packed them. More rummaging led to a triumphant yell as Jodie brandished her four-inch killer-heeled strappy sandals above her head. They would definitely make a difference, but she could hardly go out naked from the waist up. A further rummage produced her only posh top, a sleeveless red sparkly vest with a respectably high neckline that just happened to be very clingy.

"Slut," she muttered, grinning as she pulled it on, deciding against a bra.

No underwear at all? She chuckled, deciding she *had* definitely turned into a slut. No, not slutty, she told herself, but classy with an edge. She applied makeup with a light hand, and was satisfied with the way she looked. More importantly, she liked the way she felt. This was for her. This was who she was nowadays. And if the look just happened to get her laid, who was she to complain?

At five minutes to seven, she opened her bedroom door and sauntered into the main room, swinging her hips. Both guys were already there, drinking beer. They hadn't noticed her yet, so she took a moment to absorb the view, which was pretty damned hot. Milo's appearance took her breath away. In black jeans and mesh black T-shirt, black hair flopping across his brow, he looked...well, dark, deadly, dangerous—and drop-dead gorgeous. All the pent-up feelings she'd entertained for so long for this magnificent, intelligent, complex, tough, and highly infuriating enigma bubbled to the surface. *Fuck remaining detached!* She wanted this man as a permanent fixture in her life. Determination coursed through her. She was a great believer in fate. Fate had thrown them together under less than ideal circumstances, and she wasn't about to waste that opportunity.

Her glance moved on to Hal. He was wearing tight, faded blue jeans and a white shirt with the sleeves rolled back to reveal strong, tanned forearms. Sexily disheveled with his dirty-blond hair spilling across his collar, he was laughing at something he'd obviously just read in the newspaper spread across his lap. His wicked blue eyes sparkled, his gorgeous lips parted, shiny and wet. A fine tremor rocked Jodie as she observed him, making her wonder about the advisability of going without panties. Her pussy was already leaking, and she hadn't gotten much beyond her bedroom door yet. She wondered if there was something odd about her wanting them both, but didn't allow guilt to fester. Life was for living, and she had a lot of living to make up for.

"Hey, guys."

Milo looked up at the sound of her voice. She tensed when she noticed his expression was again distant as his gaze moved lazily down the length of her, and slowly up again. Then a sinfully tempting smile of approval invaded his features, and Jodie relaxed again.

"You look good enough to eat, darling." Hal jumped up to give her a hug, reached for her hand, and led her to the sofa he'd just vacated.

"Going out without knickers, Ms. Bisset." Milo shook a finger at her, an unholy light in his eye. "Whatever would Mommy say?"

"Mommy's not here." Jodie sat down and made a big deal out of crossing her legs. Both guys watched her every move intently. "And even if she was, she would be too drunk to notice."

"Glass of wine before we leave?" Hal suggested.

"Yes, please."

He got up, poured her one from the open bottle he took from the fridge, and handed it to her.

"Thanks, I could do with this."

"No bra, either," Milo said in an accusatory tone. "How can I take it off later, if you're not wearing it in the first place?"

"What makes you think I'd let you take it off, even if I was?"

"Oh, baby, you'd let me." He was disgustingly sure of himself, which infuriated Jodie, bringing out the devil in her. "Trust me on this."

Jodie inverted her chin, having fun. "Has anyone ever told you you're impossibly arrogant?"

"Many times," Hal replied for him. "He takes no notice."

"Hmm, why am I not surprised?"

"It's not arrogance, darling," Milo said smugly. "I just happen to know you like playing with us. You're hopeless and hiding your true feelings, which is good." He winked at her, and Jodie reacted all the way to her pussy. Of course she did! "We've whetted your appetite, and you can't wait to find out what happens next."

Jodie wanted to argue with him, but knew she was on to a loser. Pick your battles wisely, was one of the few useful pieces of advice her father had ever given her. This was definitely a skirmish she would never win.

"Have it your way," she contented herself with saying sweetly.

"Oh, I intend to, but how the fuck we're supposed to get through the evening and keep our hands off you when you're dressed like that, I have no fucking idea."

"Discipline, Mr. Hanson. All good things come to those who wait."

She melted when Milo fixed her with a wicked smile. "Is that right?"

He leaned forward and flicked a finger across one of her nipples. She knew they had hardened during this flirtatious exchange, but she hadn't realized they were quite so visible through her top. She glanced down, and blushed. Both men laughed at her discomfort.

"Come on, darling." Hal held out his hand and pulled her to her feet. "We've got a cab coming any time soon."

They went to an upmarket restaurant in Mayfair, owned by an ageing actor. Jodie had never been there, but had heard about it. You had to wait weeks, months even, for a reservation. How come Milo and Hal had gotten them in at such short notice? The answer soon became apparent. The highly attractive hostess appeared to know both men, and made a big thing out of kissing them, barely sparing a glance for Jodie.

"It's been too long, Milo," she said, trailing a lethally long red talon slowly down his arm. "You've been neglecting us."

"As if," he replied, winking at her.

Leave him the hell alone, he's mine!

The restaurant was full to capacity, but they were given one of the best tables—a booth with a horseshoe leather seat. Jodie slid in first and one hot man appeared on either side of her, thighs brushing against hers. Milo's hand rested on her knee beneath the table, the heat from his palm searing into her skin, and other parts of her anatomy. God, she was pathetic! He only had to touch her and her pussy leaked and throbbed.

"Don't pout, sweet thing," Milo said, amusement in his eyes. "It doesn't suit you."

"Who's pouting?" She turned away from him and smiled at Hal. "What's good here?" she asked, glancing at the menu, which was in French.

"You are," Hal replied, placing his hand on her opposite thigh and squeezing gently. *Oh my!*

Milo ordered wine, and they chose their dishes. Jodie was then free to take in her surroundings, and enjoy the ambience of a trendy restaurant in the heart of fashionable London. She adored people watching, and this place didn't disappoint. The guys pointed out famous people to her, and they laughed at some of the posing going on.

"You really should have worn panties," Milo said softly, his hand returning to rest heavily on her thigh when their appetizers had been taken away, and their glasses refilled by an attentive waiter.

"Really?" Jodie sent him a superior smile. "And why would that be?"

It was Hal who answered her. "We like challenges, and knowing we've got a beautiful lady sitting between us, not wearing any underwear, is just too damned tempting to resist."

"Sorry, boys, I'm not with you."

"Feeling damp?" Milo asked with a smoldering smile.

Hell, yes! "Not in the least."

"Liar." Milo's hand tapped her thigh hard enough to make her gasp. "Being untruthful will earn you a punishment later."

"How do you—"

"It shows in your eyes. They're hazy with desire," Milo told her. "Your nipples give you away, too."

Jodie moistened her lips, and then reached for her wineglass. Her mouth was suddenly very dry. "How observant you are."

"Drop your knees open," Milo said, his tone smoky, provocative.

Jodie was shocked by the request, but powerless to resist. Her knees splayed of their own accord, and the hand resting on her thigh worked its way higher. Jodie's breath hitched in her throat. This was *sooo* hot, but here, in the middle of a busy restaurant? Surrounded by all these people? Perhaps that was what made it so hot. Jodie hadn't realized she enjoyed an audience, but then she'd learned a lot about her sexual preferences over the last couple of days.

"Wh–what are you—"

"I'm going to play with you, darling," Milo replied. "Teach you a lesson for being such a tease." His thumb brushed just once against her swollen clit.

"Oh!" The feeling was so intense she almost elevated from the seat.

"Keep still, and take your punishment," Milo said with quiet authority. "You are *not* to come, Jodie, here in the middle of a high-end restaurant." He sent her a teasing smile. "Whatever would the owners say?"

Fuck the owners! "I wouldn't think of it," she said in a commendably even tone, given the mayhem Milo's marauding hand was causing to her body.

Hal's rich laughter caused her to look his way. "You love what Milo's doing to you, don't you, honey?"

"Yes," she replied breathlessly. There was no point in lying when she was so hopeless and concealing her reactions. "It's hot."

Milo looked so fucking relaxed, leaning back on the seat, his free hand toying with the stem of his wineglass as he relentlessly, and very expertly, agitated her clit. Holy shit, if he didn't stop, she really wouldn't be able to hold it. It was too much. Where the hell were their entrees? He'd have to stop then, wouldn't he? *Oh my.* Hal had slipped a hand beneath her butt and was squeezing her buttock.

"Guys, please!"

"Yes, Jodie, what is it?" Milo asked, infuriatingly polite. "Is something wrong?"

"This is torture. I'll do anything you like later, I promise, but either stop this right now or else let me come."

"You'll do anything we ask of you anyway, sweet thing. Still, as you ask so persuasively. What do you think, Hal?"

Hal shook his head. "Don't think she should come. You know how noisy she gets."

"I can be quiet." She didn't care if she sounded like a petulant child denied a favorite toy. They were way better at this than she was. She was so far behind the game she wasn't even on the starting bench. Heat radiated through her like thermonuclear energy. If she didn't find an outlet for it soon, she would self-combust. "Honest I can."

"You're not the only one in pain here, honey." Milo dropped his voice several octaves as he picked up her hand and placed it on his zipper. She gasped. He was enormous, throbbing and twitching, and she could feel the heat of his arousal. "See what you've done to me, and I'm betting Hal's in a similar state."

She giggled. "Sorry!"

"You will be." Milo fixed her with one of his wicked smiles. "I'm looking forward to having your sweet lips wrapped around this baby when we get home."

"It would be my pleasure. But please…argh!"

Without warning her to expect it, Milo jabbed at her pussy with what felt like all four fingers, his thumb denting the thin fabric of her pants as he made a hard, aggressive assault on her clit. It was too much. Jodie covered her mouth with her hand to prevent a scream escaping, moved her pelvis beneath the cover of the tablecloth, and fell apart.

"Did you know your eyes dilate when you come?" Hal asked, grinning at her as she returned to the land of the conscious.

"It felt like my entire body dilated. Thanks." Jodie smiled at Milo, feeling great relief, shyness, and excitement all at once. "I might be able to enjoy my dinner now."

"And here it comes," Milo said, sitting back, the epitome of calm composure, so the waiter could place the plates in front of them. How did he do that? She knew just how aroused he was. What discomfort he must be feeling. But from his demeanor, no one else in the place could possibly have a clue.

* * * *

"Come on," Milo said, collecting up his credit card and leaving a generous tip in cash on the plate. "Let's get out of here."

They stepped out of the restaurant and found a line of cabs waiting outside. They climbed into the back of one, Jodie once again sandwiched between them. Milo slid an arm around her shoulders. Hal grasped one of her hands. The game in the restaurant had been designed to test her limits, and her courage. She had surprised Milo on both counts. He knew she was sensual, and responsive, but to have the courage to actually climax in the middle of a busy restaurant took guts. Or desperation. Shit, Milo had almost come himself, just watching her. She blew his mind, and his self-control. She was going to have to pay for that. Her cute butt was in for a real pasting when they got her home.

The cab ride was fast at this time of night, the traffic thin, as though London's motorists knew how desperate Milo and Hal were to get Jodie between the sheets, and took pity on their frustrated condition. Milo shared a glance with Hal over Jodie's head, aware that his buddy's thoughts would be running along similar lines to his own. Was it too soon for them to take her at the same time?

Probably.

She'd never had anal sex before. Hell, he wanted at her arse! She'd taken to the plug like a natural, but moving on, getting her used to having her butt invaded by one of their cocks, would require patience. Jodie wasn't quite as worldly as she liked to think. Milo shook his head at Hal, telling him both together was out of the question.

Hal paid the cab, and they hustled Jodie into the building. She watched them both with a speculative light in her eye as the elevator whisked them up to the penthouse. As though they'd already discussed it, both men kept their hands to themselves in the elevator, making her wait, and wonder. She stood close to Milo, repeatedly moistening her lovely lips with the tip of her tongue. *Christ!*

"That was a lovely meal, guys, thanks," she said, walking ahead of them into the loft, swinging her hips, the little tease.

"Hey, where do you think you're going?" Hal asked when she headed for the bedrooms.

"Oh, I'm tired. I thought I'd turn in." She blew them a shared kiss. "Night."

Milo and Hal looked at one another, and then roared with laughter. She was trying to pay them back for ignoring her in the lift.

"Get back here right now, and onto your knees," Milo said in his Dom's voice.

To her credit, she remembered what to do. Perhaps it was an instinctive response to Milo's tone, but she dropped her gaze and returned to their position in front of the fireplace, falling gracefully to her knees on the thick rug.

Milo had it all planned out. She could suck his cock while Hal worked her ass. Before he could open his mouth to give her instructions, his cell phone rang.

"Shit!" Talk about lousy timing. He pulled it from his pocket, but didn't recognize the caller's number. "Hanson," he said brusquely.

"Is Jodie there, please?"

Milo frowned. "Who is this?"

"Mike Pearson."

"Just a minute." He looked down at Jodie. "Who's Mike Pearson?" he asked.

"Oh, I gave him your number. I hope you don't mind. He's making some travel arrangements for me."

"Why?" Hal frowned. "You planning on going somewhere?"

"Yes," she said, not meeting his gaze. "Islamabad."

Chapter Fourteen

"She'll call you back." Milo cut the call and glared down at Jodie, who was still kneeling on the rug. "Get up," he said curtly, anger coursing through his veins.

She did so, looking dazed and nervous, her face deathly pale. "I can explain," she said.

"This ought to be good." Hal's tone was laced with icy, incipient rage.

"Sit!" Milo pushed her toward a settee and then sat with Hal on the one facing it. If she was within his reach right now he might very well throttle her.

"I'm not a dog." Jodie tossed her head, a trace of annoyance breaking through her anxiety.

"Islamabad," Milo reminded her.

"Well, there's another group I'm involved with," she replied, addressing the remark to her folded hands.

"Actively involved?" Hal asked.

"Yes."

Milo was definitely going to throttle her. "And you didn't think to tell us about it because…"

She shrugged. "It didn't seem relevant."

"Jodie, what planet do you live on?" Anger rendered Milo's voice rough and raw. "You had plans to take yourself off to one of the world's major danger spots, and didn't think it was relevant." He ran a hand through his hair, wondering if she really was that naïve. "Geez!"

"Let her explain, Milo," Hal said quietly.

Jodie shot Hal a grateful smile, which Hal ignored. "This group is raising funds to help the Syrian refugees who are now in Pakistan, in urgent need of aid. A boatload of supplies is on its way, and I've volunteered to go over and help with the distribution, that's all."

"You've what!" Milo and Hal yelled together.

"It's perfectly safe." She lifted her chin and treated Milo to a defiant stare. "Someone has to go."

"Perfectly safe?" Milo was too mad to sit still. He couldn't remember a time when he'd been angrier with anyone, which was saying a lot. He stood up, towering over her, giving full vent to his blistering rage. "Of all the hair-brained, irresponsible…Have you lost your fucking mind?"

"I won't be going alone."

"You won't be going at all," Hal said.

"The hell I won't!"

"Jodie, I thought you had some common sense." Milo took a deep breath, endeavoring to regain some composure. That was a hard ambition to achieve, given her gross lunacy and total disregard for her own welfare. When Milo thought what could, probably would, happen to her over there, his blood ran cold. "Pakistan is a hotbed of terrorist cells."

"I know that. I'm not completely dense."

"You could have fucking fooled me. Do you know what happens to Western women who get caught interfering in places like Islamabad?"

"You're thinking kidnapped?"

Milo rolled his eyes. "The idea crossed my mind. That or worse."

"Oh, the statistics show those incidents are few and far between." She flapped a hand in careless dismissal of his concerns. "That's why they hit the news when they do happen."

Did she actually just say that? "Really?" Milo replied, scathingly.

She stood to face him, no longer looking nervous, but angry. "Yes, really. I'm not as stupid as you appear to think. I've done my research. I'll be protected. Besides, it's none of your damned business what I do."

"Do your famous statistics show how safe the daughters of prominent would-be senators are?"

"No one would know who I was," she replied, sounding a little less sure of herself.

"Darling, they'd know you were on your way before you boarded the plane," Hal said, his jaw rigid. "They probably wouldn't be able to believe their luck, or your naivety."

"I'm having trouble with that one myself." Milo ran both hands through his hair this time. "Didn't you remember what I said about not contacting any of your do-gooding friends? Not only do you disobey me, but you gave the fucking guy my cell phone number." Milo shook his head. "Fucking unbelievable."

"You told me not to use my own phone."

"And you didn't ask if you could give out my number." Milo was trembling with rage. "Grow up, Jodie. This isn't only about you."

"No, it's about the refugees, who seem to mean so little to you. And for your information, Mike isn't a do-gooder. He's just making travel arrangements for our group. I expect he's heard about my arrest and wanted to know when I'd be free to travel again."

"You are *not* going to Islamabad, Jodie, you can forget that."

"Who made you my father?" she demanded, eyes blazing. "I've already got one overcontrolling parent. I don't need another."

"Apart from the fact that you can't travel right now," Milo said through tightly clenched teeth. "I also happen to be your legal representative. It would be suicide if you went, and I have a duty to protect you against your own fucking stupidity. Do you have any idea what they do to Western women over there?"

"We already covered that." Jodie wrapped her arms around her torso and shrugged. "Besides, you're overreacting."

"Find another way to help," Hal said, defusing the tension with his quiet voice of reason. "Something less dangerous. We understand you're passionate about your causes, and we admire you for that. We just don't want to see you get hurt."

"I guess I have no choice to find another way, since I can't travel." Jodie did not look happy about that. *Tough!* "I'll only be holding the others up."

"Thank fuck."

Milo expelled a slow breath, doing his best to rein in his violent temper. When it got away from him like that, it scared him. Still, on this occasion he had justification to get mad. Her rank stupidity, thinking she could swan around the world, righting all its wrongs single-handed, would anger a better man than he'd ever be. His blood ran cold when he considered the most likely outcome, had she made it to Islamabad. He realized at that moment just how much she'd come to mean to him over the past couple of days, accounting for his violent reaction to her foolishness. Hell would freeze over before he allowed her to doing something so stupid. Handcuffing her to his bed for the next six months suddenly seemed like a good way to keep her in line.

"You sure know how to kill the mood," he said softly, his temper evaporating as he visualized her naked and shackled, at his complete mercy.

"I don't want to argue with you, Milo," Jodie replied. "We obviously won't ever see eye to eye on this topic, and since I can't go, there's no point talking about it." She turned away from him. "I think I'd better go to bed."

Milo nodded. "I think that's a good idea."

His phone rang again. Thinking it was Jodie's travel agent, he took the call without checking the caller ID, ready to tell the guy to take a hike.

"Mr. Hanson, it's Bisset here."

Shit, Jodie's father. That was all he needed. "How can I help you?" he asked curtly, remembering how badly their last conversation had gone, and in no mood to speak to the tyrant right now.

"Is Jodie there? I need an urgent word."

"Just a moment." He put the call on hold and nodded to Jodie. "It's your father. I'll put him on speaker."

"He hasn't got anything to say to me that you need to hear."

"Even so." He pressed the speakerphone button. "Jodie's right here," he said.

"Jodie?"

"Dad, what's up?" Jodie shared a worried frown between Milo and Hal, which is when Milo realized that Bisset didn't sound like his normal bombastic self.

"It's your mom, honey." He sounded as though he was only just holding it together. "There's no easy way to tell you this."

"Tell me what, Dad? You're worrying me."

"I'm sorry, baby, but this afternoon your mom tried to take her own life."

"Oh my god!" Jodie clasped a hand over her mouth. "I thought she'd gotten better."

"She'd been doing fine. I think perhaps the pressure of the campaign tipped her over the edge. It's all my fault." His voice cracked. "I've put too much pressure on her. I know how fragile she is. I never should have—"

"What happened?"

"She overdosed on her sleeping meds. Fortunately I came home unexpectedly and caught her in time. She's gone back into rehab."

"Is she in the usual place?"

"No, honey. It's a new facility." Hal handed Jodie a pen and piece of paper, and she jotted down the address. "No visitors for several days, though. She has to be given time to stabilize and start therapy before she sees anyone from the outside world."

"Can't I at least call to find out how she is?"

"Sure you can. You have the number. But you can call me. I'll be kept informed."

"I'm sorry, Dad." There were tears in Jodie's eyes. His anger with her now completely forgotten, Milo slipped an arm around her shoulders. She leaned her head against his chest, eyes briefly closed, tears seeping from beneath her lashes. Instead of the tough campaigner she wanted the world to see, she was now a little girl, alone and vulnerable in a foreign country, sideswiped by her dysfunctional parents, unsure what to do. Milo's heart broke for her. "Will she be all right?"

"I…I don't know."

"I'd come home, but I can't travel. This stupid arrest thing."

"I could really do with you here, darling. Perhaps, if it gets cleared up, you could—"

"Is Paul with you? Does he know?"

"He knows, but there's nothing he can do."

"He could support you."

"I'm okay. Paul has responsibilities. He can't just…"

Milo tuned out, wondering where this was leading. There was something not quite right about it, but he couldn't put his finger on what was bugging him. Jodie finished her conversation with her father, having promised to return to the States the moment she was free to travel.

"Looks like you've gotten your wish," she said, flashing Milo a watery smile. "I definitely won't be going to Islamabad now."

Before Milo could respond, his phone rang again. This time he did check the display, and took the call.

"Raoul, how's it going?"

As he listened, the pieces fell into place. What he hadn't been able to figure out about Bisset was now crystal clear.

"Yeah, that makes perfect sense," he said, grinding his jaw.

"That's what I figured. Talk to Jodie about it and let me know what you decide to do."

"Will do. Oh, and Raoul, can you do me a favor. Jodie's mom has been taken into rehab." Milo reeled off the address. "Can you check on her status for me?"

"Sure thing. What are you thinking, buddy?"

"I'll let you know when you get back to me."

"Fair enough."

Jodie and Hal were both looking at him when he hung up. "Why did you ask Raoul to check on Mom?" Jodie asked. "Dad's already given us a report on her condition."

Milo shrugged. "It's probably nothing. Just a gut feeling."

"What did Raoul want?" Hal asked.

"He's identified the guy who took your picture outside the nick," Milo replied, sliding an arm around her waist.

"Oh, who is he?" Jodie asked.

"He's a Yank who works for a senatorial campaign."

Jodie nodded. "It's as we thought. Someone's done this to me to undermine Dad."

"No, sweetheart." Milo swallowed. There was no easy way to tell her this. "The guy actually works for your father."

* * * *

Jodie's mouth fell open, and she couldn't seem to close it again. She heard voices saying her name, expressing concern about her, but they seemed to be coming from a long distance away. Her head spun, her stomach lurched, and her knees trembled so violently they were unable to support her weight. Milo's strong arms caught her just before she crumbled to the floor.

"Come and sit down, darling." His tone was gentle, caressing— very different from the contemptuous anger that had ripped through her like a knife just moments ago. "You've had a shock. Rest your head between your knees and take a moment."

"I'm okay."

"You don't look it." Hal hovered on her other side, an anxious frown creasing his brow. "Let me get you some water."

She lifted her head when Hal returned with the water. At least the world was no longer spinning. She sat back, sipping the water, a hot man on either side of her, watching her closely. She felt a little better now. As the shock wore off, it was replaced with a slow, virulent anger that burned its way through her insides like an incurable disease.

"He's responsible for everything, isn't he?" Jodie knew it was true, but still had trouble believing it. "Everything that's happened, my own father did it to me."

Milo's eyes bore into hers, and she could sense he had transferred his anger from her to her father, where it belonged. She had her caring, compassionate, devastatingly proficient Milo back, fighting in her corner. And Hal, too. His reassuring presence, the feel of his hand squeezing hers, gave her hope. She needed them, both of them, and they were telling her without the need for words that they were there for her.

"Looks that way," Milo said, grinding his jaw.

"I knew he was controlling, and ambitious. I also knew he hated me not doing what he wanted me to, but I never would have thought he would stoop this low." She glanced at Milo, then at Hal. "You guys don't look totally surprised."

"I'm not." Milo compressed his lips into a thin, hard line. "Something didn't seem quite right about your arrest from the first. Those papers were so damned obvious. No self-respecting terrorist group would leave that sort of shit hanging around, or even commit it to paper in the first place."

"He was prepared for me to be arrested, humiliated, worried out of my mind, just so he could—" Jodie blinked. "Could what?"

"I'll bet my bank balance an explanation for the plans will show up tomorrow, and all charges will be dropped, now that you've agreed to go home to your Mom, of course," Hal said with a cynical twist to his lips.

"You won't get many takers," Milo replied. "I guess he wants you back so you can take your mom's place on the campaign trail, just like you always thought. That's what this has been about all along. Your mom is fragile, he can't guarantee she won't fall off the wagon and embarrass him by saying or doing something out of place. You, on the other hand, are young, fresh, and beautiful—the perfect American daughter." Jodie made a scoffing sound at the back of her throat. "You're his ticket to the senate, darling. His ace in the hole."

"That's what he's wanted all along, but I wouldn't play nice." Jodie shook her head. "But now I don't have a lot of choice, not with Mom the way she is."

"*If* she is," Milo said softly.

Jodie's head shot up, tears brimming, but she stubbornly refused to allow them to fall. "What do you mean?"

"Well, he tried to get you to say you'd go home as soon as the charges were dropped, but you wouldn't commit. That didn't work, so he had to try something more drastic. He knows you feel more connection to your mother than you do to him, despite her alcoholism, or perhaps because of it. I suspect, in your heart, you believe she is the way she is because of your father's controlling ways. Am I right?" Jodie nodded. "She needs to be treated with kid gloves. Your roles have reversed, but you still feel some empathy for her, even if she was a crap mother."

"Yes, but he wouldn't force an overdose on her, just to get me back. That's taking things too far."

Milo flexed a brow. "Wouldn't he? You know him better than I do, but personally, I'd say there's not much he wouldn't do to get you back where he wants you."

"No, you're wrong, and there's an easy way to prove it," Jodie said decisively. "I can call the number Dad gave me for the clinic, and ask how Mom's doing."

"You could," Milo replied, "but that won't help. All you'll get is a professional person answering the phone, telling you what he wants you to hear."

"I don't believe what you're saying. I don't like my father very much, don't approve of his methods, but he definitely wouldn't go that far." Jodie widened her eyes. "How could he make it happen, even if he wanted to?"

Milo sent her a tender look that melted her vulnerable heart. What she would give to see that look directed at her every day, for the rest of her life. "He was willing to have you arrested as a terrorist. That must have taken some organization, and a lot of risk, to pull it off. You think he can't set up a fake phone number for a clinic?"

"Well, I...hell, I just don't know what to think."

"He said no visitors or direct phone contact with your mom for a few days, hoping you'd be back with him within that time frame."

"If I was, how would he explain Mom being home, alive and well?"

"He said she took an overdose, remember," Milo replied.

"Yes, but Mom would know she didn't."

"Would she?" Milo's intelligent gaze rested on her face. "You said yourself she doesn't know which way is up, half the time. Your father will just gloss over it all, saying it wasn't as bad as it seemed. Or he might even have her sent to rehab somewhere."

"He's right, babe." Hal shrugged. "Men like your father with money, ambition, and influence can get away with just about anything. Or they think they can."

"But we don't know for absolutely sure." Jodie twisted her fingers together, unwilling, in spite of her ambivalent feelings toward her father, to accept the blindingly obvious.

"We soon will. Raoul's having someone check out the physical location of the facility, rather than just phoning the number your dad gave us. We'll know by morning, but I'd bet the farm on being right."

"And I wouldn't bet against Milo," Hal added, his grin lightening the somber mood. "That's never a good plan."

Jodie wouldn't, either. She had a sudden, unshakable feeling that Milo was spot-on. Anger hazed her vision. Disillusionment dulled her mind. And, astonishingly, a deep, disturbing bolt of desire ripped through her. Talk about lousy timing!

"Hey, babe." Milo cupped her chin with his long fingers. "We've beaten him. You don't have to dance to his tune anymore."

"I never did, that's what caused this mess in the first place. My beloved father can't bear to have anyone go against his wishes. Control freaks don't come more tightly wired than him."

"Would you like something stronger than water to help with the shock?" Hal asked.

"No." She sat up straight, looking at them both with determination. "What I'd like is to go to bed. With both of you."

Chapter Fifteen

"Are you sure, babe?"

Milo shared a glance with Hal, who shrugged. He obviously didn't understand her reaction any better than Milo did. Or there again, perhaps they were all on the same page here. Whenever he and Hal had been in dangerous situations in the service, getting drunk or, better yet, getting laid, had always seemed like a good way to blot it all out. Jodie was living for the moment, and they owed it to her to help her out.

"Must be your lucky day," she said, a little too carelessly.

"You've had a shock. You might regret it in the morning."

"Milo Hanson, I've been lusting after you for a decade." She inhaled sharply and wagged a finger at him. "You can close your mouth, and stop looking so smug. I just need to get you out of my system, and learn a little bit more about this sharing jag that you guys have running, then I'll leave you both in peace."

Milo pretended to be affronted. "You just want us for our bodies?"

"Damned straight I do!" She looked up at him, tears still swamping her remarkable eyes. But an enigmatic smile flirted with her lips, as though she'd just realized she really did hold the whip hand, figuratively speaking.

"Well, in that case, who are we to deny a lady what she wants?"

"Couldn't have put it better myself," Hal said, blowing Jodie a kiss.

Milo leaned down, grabbed her face between his hands, and kissed her like he meant business, which he did. He broke the kiss again quickly, leaving her breathless. He then swept her from the sofa, straight into his arms, and carried her toward the bedrooms.

"Seems she's already forgotten all the stuff we taught her," he said to Hal. "I don't see any signs of submissive obedience, do you, pal?"

"Can't say as I do," Hal replied, opening Milo's bedroom door for him.

He deposited Jodie on his bed, still wearing her tight pants and sexy top. She leaned back on her elbows, and looked up at them both, smoldering desire replacing her earlier tears.

"How far do you want to take this, babe?" Milo asked. "It's your call."

"I'll leave you to set the parameters. All I ask is that you take me out of myself. I just want to forget all about the past few days, about my manipulating father in particular, and have some fun." Her eyes glistened. "And I don't want you to make any allowances for my relative inexperience."

Milo and Hal exchanged a speaking glance.

"Okay, but if you don't like something, just remember the safety word."

"I doubt that will be necessary." Sexual tension fuelled the air, palpable and pulsating, as she gazed up at them. "I'm at your mercy, gentlemen."

Shit! "Stand up and remove your clothes," Milo said curtly.

Jodie was naked in seconds. She remained standing, eyes downcast, trembling with anticipation. At least, he hoped that was what had made her tremble. She had removed her collar before they went out to dinner. Hal popped to her room, found it on the dresser, and returned with it.

"Here we go, darling," he said, fixing it around her neck again. "That's better."

"Go and kneel in the corner with your back to us," Milo ordered. "We need to talk about this without you looking on."

"We need to do something about that cute butt of hers," Hal said softly once she'd complied. "You piqued her curiosity this afternoon."

"That's what I figured. You take her arse, and she can suck me off at the same time."

"No, mate, you can do the honors." Hal grinned. "She already gave me head once, and I gotta say, I don't mind going down that route again."

Milo thought about it for a moment, relieved that Hal had made the suggestion, wondering if he'd done so for Milo's sake. Jodie wouldn't be able to see him if he was behind her and she was on all fours, which suited Milo just fine. He didn't know what madness had persuaded him to reveal himself in all his ugly glory to her the night before. It wouldn't happen again. Jodie had managed to disguise her reaction pretty damned well, but he wasn't ready to talk about it to her, or to suffer her sympathy. Anything but that, and Hal would know it.

"Okay, that'll work," Milo said.

"You gonna spank her first?"

"No, I laid into her pretty hard this afternoon. I'm betting her backside's still sore. I saw her wince once or twice when she shifted position in the restaurant."

"Okay, let's do this."

They turned to look at her, and both inhaled sharply. She was waggling her butt in the air, and playing with one of her nipples. Gross misconduct that would normally earn her a big punishment. Today it simply stoked the guys' fires.

"Stop that, Jodie!" Milo said in an authoritative tone.

"Sorry, Sir. I was feeling kinda neglected, and needy."

"Go get on the bed, on your hands and knees. Keep your eyes down and don't look at us."

* * * *

Both men had shed their clothes as soon as she was in position. Jodie knew she wasn't supposed to look at them, but they were so handsome, so strong, muscular, so every damned thing, that not stealing a peek was beyond her. She suspected they noticed, but cut her some slack. Shame that, she wouldn't have minded being punished. She kinda liked taking Milo's spankings. Crouching naked in the corner and feeling their admiring gazes fixed on her had been a real turn-on. Who would have thought it?

Now her problems had been resolved, this might well be her swansong with the guys. She'd caused them more than enough trouble, and they'd want her out of here so they could have their privacy back. Okay, Jodie could be grown up about that, and would leave without protest. But in the meantime she'd take her fun any which way they were prepared to hand it out.

Hal slid beneath her sideways and applied his lips to her nipples—sucking, teasing, and biting. Molding and caressing with his skilled fingers at the same time, forcing her solidified nipples deeper into his mouth. Oh, his magical lips! This sort of divine torture she could get used to. Needy little mewling sounds slipped past her lips when he fastened his teeth around one puckered nipple and tugged. Hard. Fires ignited in her belly, and she cried out, wishing she could reach out and caress his muscular torso, run her hands across his washboard abs, and return in some small way the pleasure he was giving her. She couldn't, not if she was to hold her position for Milo. Damn it, they were *sooo* mean to her!

After a few minutes, she felt the bed dip as Milo climbed into his favorite position behind her. His hot body pressed above hers as he leaned over, pushed her hair aside, and trailed damp kisses across her nape, making her shiver when he tugged on her collar at the same time. He continued across her shoulders and down her spine, lapping and nipping at a different pace to which Hal was tormenting her tits. Each was equally arousing. She squirmed against Milo's lips, muttering beneath her breath as Hal continued to agitate her nipples.

The feel of them both touching her, their large capable hands sweeping across her most intimate places, caused shards of pleasure to blast her body from all angles. A paradox of pleasure and longing swept through her, so powerful, so intense, it stunned her senses.

"Responsive little thing, ain't she?" Milo remarked, bringing his hand down lightly over her backside.

Harder, Master, please.

He resumed kissing and biting his way down her spine, continuing to caress her buttocks with one hand, occasionally sliding a finger down her crack. The distraction of Hal's teeth on her nipples meant she barely felt the discomfort, and managed not to flinch when his fingers became more invasive.

"I've never had an arse virgin before," he said in a sexy whisper that sent renewed shivers down the spine he was still kissing. "Need to make this special for you, babe."

"You already are," she replied breathlessly.

Jodie was getting impatient. There was such a thing as too much foreplay. She squirmed against Hal's teeth and Milo's lips, finding it increasingly difficult to hold her position. Milo slid a hand beneath her buttocks, and she heard a sharp intake of his breath, followed by a deep, rich chuckle.

"You really are ready, aren't you, sugar."

"Yes, Sir."

Well, there wasn't much point in denying it. Honey trickled down the insides of her thighs for them both to see and feel. She flinched when Milo squirted something cold over her backside—lube, presumably. She gasped, and instinctively shrunk away from it.

"Keep still." He administered a gentle rap. "You wanted this, darling, but there's still time to change my mind."

"No chance!"

Milo's throaty laugh caused all the muscles in her belly to clench. How did he do that to her? "Just checking," he said, his breath warm and moist against her shoulder.

Damn it, this was hot! Jodie was panting, leaking, and totally turned on. Milo rubbed the lube into her backside with large sweeps of his hand, concentrating on the crack between her buttocks, and gently easing a slick finger into her anus. She tensed up immediately.

"Let me in, sugar," he crooned softly in her ear. "Trust me, it'll blow your mind."

Hal had a small vibrator that he slid into her cunt. Oh, the sharp buzz was as unexpected as it was welcome. It distracted her, and Milo's finger found its way past her coiled muscle.

"Ah, you see, you really do want this."

She mumbled something that made no sense, because the last thing she wanted right now was to be sensible. Jodie wiggled her arse, incapable of keeping still in the light of the cataclysmic rush of sensation surging through her overheated body. Milo slapped her buttocks and she stopped moving at once. Knowing him, he would quit what he was doing altogether if she failed to do as she was told. Jodie wasn't prepared to take the risk.

"You're gonna have to learn to keep still, darling," he said in a reproving tone. "Remember who's in charge here. It's your duty to please us."

"Yes, Sir. I'll sure try."

"Oh, you'll do better than that, darling."

Milo started moving his finger in and out of her backside. She moved with him, still mumbling, inarticulate, filled with an inexorable longing that made her tremble with need.

"We need to get this on," Milo said, an edge to his voice, as though his self-control was also in danger of unraveling.

Presumably the statement was addressed to Hal, not her. He released the nipple he'd been tormenting and shifted his position. Jodie heard the sound of a foil packet tearing. At last!

"No need," she said breathlessly. "I'm on the pill."

"You sure?" Milo asked.

"Yeah." She panted the word. "I want to feel you."

Milo leaned down and gently bit at her buttock. "You got it, babe."

With infinite-seeming care he eased the tip of his cock into her anus.

"Fuck that feels so damned good," he said, his voice raw with passion.

"Time to play, Hal," he said from beneath her.

"No!"

"What's up, sweetheart?" Hal asked. "You don't wanna suck my cock?"

"Yes, but not now. I want it inside me, same time as Milo is."

"Ain't gonna happen, darling," Milo said from behind. "You need to get used to one thing at a time."

"Stop treating me like a child. I want to do this. I might never get another chance."

"Jodie, it's dangerous if you don't know what you're—"

"You know what to do, Milo, and I trust you." Jodie screwed up her eyes, determined to get what she wanted from these two gorgeous specimens. "Please!"

"Well, okay, if you're sure. But if gets too much, say the word."

Jodie caught Hal's grin as he slid completely beneath her, their faces more or less level. He removed the vibrator, and resumed torturing her tits.

"You need to keep absolutely still, darling, and let us do all the moving," Milo said. "If you don't we might hurt you. Do you understand?"

"Yes, hell yes. Just do it."

Milo chuckled. "With pleasure."

Milo took a firm hold of Jodie's hips. "You've shown a serious inability to keep still," he said, his lips brushing her ear, flaming her blood. "Can't risk you doing the same thing now. This is a delicate operation that requires discipline and precision."

"I understand," she said breathlessly. *Just get on with it!*

"Okay, mate, let's do this."

At last!

Without preamble, Hal sank into Jodie's pussy, hard and deep. The moment he withdrew again, Milo sank a little deeper into her backside. It felt gloriously erotic, and Jodie felt as though she was floating on an endless tide of pleasure as the two of them worked her like a well-oiled machine.

"You all right, darling?" Milo asked.

"Hmm, I had no idea."

"Babe, you ain't seen nothing yet."

"Then show me."

Milo and Hal did just that. She could sense their growing desperation as the three of them got into the zone, the sexual magnetism between them shooting off the scale.

"Shit, guys, this feels hot!"

Milo groaned and picked up the pace, filling her backside with his throbbing cock.

"Tell me how it feels," Milo said, his tone teasingly provocative, as he sank balls-deep into her arse. "I need to know."

"Like I'm being ripped in two. Like my body's combusting. Like I'm truly alive."

"Shit!" Hal said from beneath her.

"I'm close, gentlemen. You're driving me wild. I can't hold it."

"Come for us, darling," Milo said. "Let it go."

Even with Milo holding her hips, she managed to start moving on her own, greedily feeding from first one cock, then the other. She threw her head back, tortured by part pain, part pleasure, the dividing line a gloriously erotic blur as her insides liquefied.

She screamed as the guys branded her with their burning cocks and her body went into spasm. She bucked her hips between them, desperate to take as much of them both as they were willing to give her. When Milo's grunts and guttural moans became louder, more tortured, she sensed he was losing the battle to hold himself back. Hal swore, and let himself go, pouring an endless stream of hot sperm deep into her pussy. A low, animalistic sound slipped past Milo's lips as he wound her hair around one fist, pulling hard on it as he did the same thing from behind.

"Oh sweet darling," he muttered, laughing as he and Hal both withdrew and the three of them lay flat on their backs, bathed in perspiration, breathing hard. Milo leaned up on one elbow and examined her face closely. "You okay?" he asked, gently kissing the end of her nose.

Jodie wanted to laugh aloud. She was more than all right. She'd never felt more alive in her entire life. What they'd just done to her had been beyond her wildest imaginings, and several minutes later all her nerves endings still sang an operatic chorus, backed by a full orchestra and glittering starburst of fireworks.

"That was...well, words fail me." She shared a smug smile between them. "Thank you seems pretty inadequate."

"Hey, we're the ones should be thanking you," Hal replied. "Especially since you let us go bareback."

"That's what made it even better," she replied. "The feel of your cocks was...well, frictacious."

"Frictacious?" Milo grinned at her. "Is that a word?"

"It is now. What I meant was the friction of your skin inside me, was—"

"We know what you mean, sugar." Hal placed a gentle kiss on her lips. "I'll go get the shower running."

Milo remained where he was, damaged leg away from her, the lighting too dim for Jodie to see it properly.

"Shower's going to waste," Hal called.

Jodie got up, expecting Milo to join her. He didn't, which made her scowl.

"You coming?" she asked.

"You go ahead with Hal," he replied, sounding evasive. "I'll be right there."

But Jodie knew he wouldn't be, and his reticence spoiled her euphoric mood. He'd closed down on her again, and she didn't know how to reach him. As she and Hal showered together, she heard the tap running in the bathroom, and figured Milo was cleaning himself up at the basin.

"What's he doing?" she asked Hal.

Hal shrugged. "He has major issues with his leg."

"But yesterday, he—"

"He's never done that before." Hal shrugged. "Guess he's not ready to do it again yet."

"We'll see about that!"

When she and Hal returned to the bedroom, Milo was back in bed, hands folded behind his head, sheet pulled up to his waist. Jodie glowered at him.

"Problem?" he asked.

"Oh, I don't have any problems," she replied with a sweetly sarcastic smile. "But you sure as hell do."

He wouldn't meet her gaze. "Sorry, I'm not with you."

"What was all that trust bullshit you kept on spouting just now?"

"Don't curse."

"I'll say whatever I damned well please." She placed her hands on her hips, not caring that she was towering over him like a harpy—a naked, exceedingly angry harpy. "You wanted me to trust you, and I just did. Don't think there's anything a woman can do in a bedroom that shows greater trust than what I just did with you guys."

"What's your point?"

"My point is you'll only fuck me from behind, so I can't see you, or else you blindfold me. Neither option is acceptable." Milo looked shocked, but Jodie was too angry to care if she was out of line. "Okay, so you've got a war wound. Get over yourself. I love every square inch of you, Milo, scars and all, and you have absolutely nothing to be ashamed of."

He sent her a wary glance. "What is it that you're asking me to do, Jodie?"

"I'm asking for your complete and absolute trust." She impatiently brushed a tear from her cheek. "My father never trusted me, my mother was seldom sober enough to trust anyone." She shook her head. "I've spent all these years thinking you would be different. Seems I was wrong."

"You really have been thinking about me all these years." A cautious smile lifted the corners of his mouth. "You love me?"

"Both of you, as it happens, otherwise I wouldn't have done what I just did."

A second tear took the place of the first. Then another joined the party. How humiliating was it to make such an admission, and receive nothing in response, other than identical drop-jawed expressions of disbelief. She hadn't expected them to respond precisely, but they did need to know how she felt. Time wasn't on her side and she was through with playing games.

"Don't cry, darling," Milo said softly. "I hate to see you cry."

It was her turn not to respond, and the silence in the tension-filled room sucked the atmosphere dry. Milo knew what she wanted, what she needed from him. The rest was up to him. It was time to lay his neuroses to rest, and if he felt anything for her at all, he'd do the right thing. Hal, she suspected, knew it was Milo's call, which was why he'd remained silent—shocked to the core by her stupid admission of love, obviously—but silent.

Her breath hitched in her throat when, after several brittle seconds, not removing his gaze from her face, Milo pushed the sheet down with agonizing slowness. His own breathing was rapid, as though he was waiting for her to reject him. *Not gonna happen!* Triumph ripped through her as she slid onto the bed and straddled his body.

"Hands above your head," she said with authority. "Grip the headboard and don't let go, or there will be consequences."

She knew he liked to be in charge, but sensed on this occasion he'd let her run the show. With the slow, sexy smile that so got to her, he raised his hands and gripped the iron headboard.

"It's not a pretty sight, darling," he said, anxiety in his tone.

"Allow me to be the judge of that."

Slowly, Jodie did to him what he'd just done to her back, and worked her way down his torso, kissing and nipping as she went. She elicited a sharp intake of breath from Milo when she circled one of his nipples with her tongue, and then tugged at it between her teeth. Hal jumped onto the bed, caressing Jodie's butt as she leaned over and continued to deal with the cause of Milo's paranoia.

She had reached his navel now. It was time.

Slowly, sending constant glances at his face from beneath her lashes, she applied her tongue to the top of his scar. He elevated from the bed, but stilled again almost immediately, and didn't remove his hands from the headboard.

"Good boy," she said approvingly, sitting up and licking her lower lip with the tip of her tongue. "You sure do taste mighty fine."

"Christ!" Hal muttered, sounding shocked, either by Milo's passivity or because he was letting her do this. He shouldn't have been. Hal had already received the benefit of her tongue on his cock. She could use it just as efficiently on other body parts, she figured, especially damaged areas in dire need of her soft, healing touch.

She continued to lap at every tiny part of Milo's poor, damaged thigh. Her heart almost broke when she thought of all the pain he must have endured, especially when he'd only been trying to help the woman who did this to him.

"There," she said, sitting back on her heels when she'd completed her task, conscious of his throbbing erection, primed and ready for action. Again. "All better."

"The hell it is!" Milo's petrified expression gave way to a growl of frustration. He removed his hands from the headboard and, quick as a flash, lifted her from his torso, repositioning her above his cock. "Finish what you started, wench!"

She threw back her head and laughed triumphantly. "With the greatest of pleasure."

Chapter Sixteen

With Jodie sandwiched between him and Hal, her hand resting on his injured thigh, Milo slept better than he had for years. They woke their gorgeous little sub with their morning erections, and Milo finally got to feel her magical lips around his cock, while Hal got acquainted with her backside. Milo's mind went into overdrive as he thought of the things she'd said and done the night before. Had she meant them?

He hadn't been surprised when, shortly after breakfast, he received a call from Paddington Green, saying no charges would be pressed against any of those arrested. He was even less surprised when Raoul called to say the clinic where Jodie's mother was supposed to be didn't exist.

He and Hal had an urgent conversation while Jodie was in her room, packing, ready to leave. They'd told her she needed to stay a bit longer, get her mind clear, but she wouldn't hear of it. Nor would she tell them what her plans were.

"We can't let her go, pal," Hal said.

"I agree."

Hal blinked. "You do?"

"She's the one. You think I would have let anyone else touch my thigh?"

"But how are we going to stop her? She's hurting pretty bad right now, and will probably go off and do something stupid, just to get back at her old man." Hal shuddered. "Just the thought of her anywhere near Islamabad…"

"That ain't gonna happen," Milo replied, grinding his jaw.

"Then you'd better think of a way to stop her. Fast."

Jodie appeared in the main room, bringing their conversation to an end.

"Come and sit down, babe," Milo said. "We need to talk to you."

It was another hot day. Milo was wearing shorts again, but this time they were short enough to show part of his scar. Somehow it didn't seem to matter anymore.

"What are your plans, darling?" Hal asked.

"Well, I'm not going back to the States. I can't even bring myself to talk to my father." She tossed her head. "I'll only say something I'd later regret if I do. Let the bastard stew."

"Ata girl!" Milo smiled at her, then lifted her up and deposited her on his lap. "Tell me again that bit about having loved me for years."

"And loving me as much as you do him," Hal added, grinning.

"Oh, that was just said to get your attention."

"You succeeded." Milo massaged her back with large sweeps of one hand. "But I was hoping there might be an element of truth in it."

She blinked. "You were?"

"Hmm."

"Why?"

"Because Hal and I would like you to stay here with us." Milo brushed his lips against hers. "Permanently."

"You're kidding me?" Her mouth formed a perfect O. "Don't joke about such things."

"We're deadly serious," Hal said, taking her hand.

"Right." Milo nodded emphatically. "We didn't think we wanted or needed a permanent woman in our lives, but it didn't take us two minutes to realize you were different. I think that's what confused me for a while. I was a jerk, the way I behaved. I'm sorry, babe." He touched her face, sliding his index finger across her lips. "We're both in love with you, and don't want to let you go."

"But what about…well, you know." She touched Milo's exposed scar. "You know what it is that I want to do, and I know how you feel about it."

"You taught me something important about myself last night," Milo said, kissing her hairline. "I've been way too sensitive. There are people a lot worse off than me."

"But we can't have you taking yourself off to Pakistan," Hal said sternly. "We care about you too much to let that happen."

"However," Milo added, tag-teaming Hal in an effort to get her to see reason. "I've been making some enquiries this morning. I know you don't want to work for one of the big charities, and I can't say I blame you for that. Way too much bureaucracy. But there's a smaller one, officially registered, that's just been set up in this country to help young girls in Africa, saving them from abuse and underage marriage."

"Go on," she said slowly.

"It just so happens that they have a vacancy for a fundraising manager. It will require a lot of PR expertise, public speaking, that sort of stuff, and the salary sucks. But still, I thought it might—""

"Yes!" Jodie flung her arms around Milo's neck, then leaned down from her perch on his knee to kiss Hal's lips deeply. "Yes, to both suggestions. I love you both, and I absolutely don't want to leave you. I just thought you wouldn't want me hanging around any longer, cramping your style."

"Darling," Milo replied, caressing her with his eyes. "You can cramp any parts of us you like!"

* * * *

Back in Wyoming, Raoul hung up the phone and shrugged at Zeke.

"Remind me never to send our operatives in where a pretty woman's involved," he said huffily.

"Why, what's happened now?"

"Seems Milo and Hal have persuaded Jodie to move in with them. Permanently. That was her father on the phone, tearing me a new one for letting it happen."

"Don't suppose his political ambitions will survive the fall-out, if his opponents get to hear about it," Zeke replied chuckling.

Raoul curled his lip. "After the stunt he tried to pull, the bastard doesn't deserve a political career."

"No, I'm guessing he'll have to withdraw." Zeke's grin was positively lethal. "Because I have a strange premonition the press will get to hear how he arranged his daughter's arrest for his own selfish purposes, if he still tries to run, that is."

Raoul pretended surprise. "Whoever would do that to him?"

"I can't begin to imagine," Zeke replied, still grinning.

THE END

WWW.ZARACHASE.COM

ABOUT THE AUTHOR

Zara Chase is a British author who spends a lot of her time travelling the world. Being a gypsy provides her with ample opportunities to scope out exotic locations for her stories. She likes to involve her heroines in her erotic novels in all sorts of dangerous situations—and not only with the hunky heroes whom they encounter along the way. Murder, blackmail, kidnapping and fraud—to name just a few of life's more common crimes— make frequent appearances in her books, adding pace and excitement to her racy stories.

Zara is an animal lover who enjoys keeping fit and is on a one-woman mission to keep the wine industry ahead of the recession.

For all titles by Zara Chase, please visit
www.bookstrand.com/zara-chase

Siren Publishing, Inc.
www.SirenPublishing.com

CPSIA information can be obtained at www.ICGtesting.com
Printed in the USA
LVOW04s1041140415

434402LV00036B/2042/P